COFFIN FALLS: THE DAY THE DOME FELL
Copyright © 2026 by Trena Cannon

ISBN: 979-8-9932613-2-4

Cover Design by Brittany Evans @ BEDESIGNS.CA

Edited and Formatted by Represent Publishing & Kelsey Darling

COFFIN FALLS

THE DAY THE DOME FELL

COFFIN FALLS

THE DAY THE DOME FELL

BOOK 1

TRENA CANNON

Represent Publishing

DEDICATION

For my editor, Chelsea, who showed extraordinary patience through edits and treatment alike. Thank you for your grace and compassion during my hardest year.

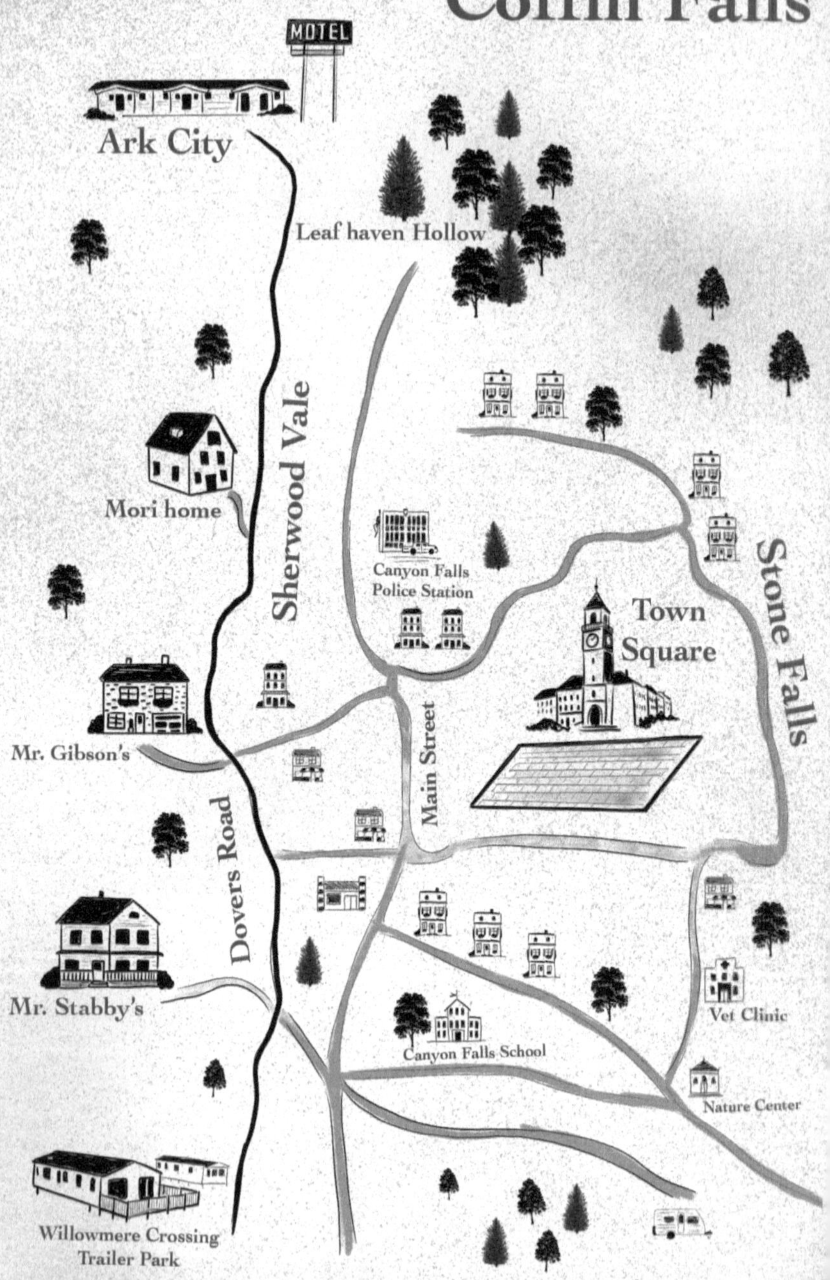

Coffin Falls
MOTEL
Ark City
Leaf haven Hollow
Sherwood Vale
Mori home
Canyon Falls Police Station
Town Square
Stone Falls
Mr. Gibson's
Main Street
Dovers Road
Mr. Stabby's
Vet Clinic
Canyon Falls School
Nature Center
Willowmere Crossing Trailer Park

CHAPTER ONE
FRIDAY, 12:55 P.M.

AMY

A sharp, persistent ringing jolts me upright as books slam shut. Chairs scrape against linoleum, and chatter grows louder with conversation. I glance above the whiteboard. Class is over. I stretch myself fully awake and lower my gaze to Mr. Hawkins. He's standing behind his desk shouting out our assignment for the weekend, but no one is listening. Most have already left the classroom and are screaming down the hall in excitement.

Tonight is our first football game of the year, and everyone is practically foaming at the mouth to go. Which is stupid. Canyon Falls is so tiny; it can't even scrape enough students together for a JV team, so everyone plays Varsity. Even some of the freshmen are starters, whether they are ready or not. I sort of feel bad for them. I mean, they're barely out of the peewee league and get tossed into a brutal game. You'd think their parents would have something to say about it, but they have the football rabies too. They even go as far as throwing money at the coach. I should know; my twin brother, Shin, used to be on the team. And if all that isn't bad enough, the school is releasing us early so we can prepare for the game. Sorry— get hyped up for the game.

I slowly gather my things, watching the room empty until only a few students are left.

So, when I say everyone goes to the games, I mean *everyone*. It doesn't matter what the weather is or if it's out of town. It's almost a sin not to attend. This is Texas. The football capital of the world. At least that's what every dumb boy here says. Hell, even the minister at my church adds a prayer at the end of his service, hoping God will play a hand in their next game. It's ridiculous. And if you're not on the football team, a cheerleader, or dating someone from that clique, you sort of disappear into the background.

I push to my feet, lugging my heavy backpack over my shoulder, and start for the door, only to find a few football players crowded together, blocking my way.

"Excuse me." When they don't look at me or move, I force myself through two linebackers and straight into Hell.

The hall is a complete madhouse. Worse than usual. The air is suffocating with too much perfume and over-powering cologne. Plus, there's crap everywhere like it's the last week of school, instead of the first. Paper and trash litter the hall, along with the hand-painted posters that have been taped on the walls all week. Most of the lockers are decorated in our school colors. Green and gold. And not just for the football players. Everyone. After all, we're all a team here. Gooo, Bulldogs!

Gross!

Someone barrels by, shoving me right into the town flyer, Robby Jensen. The stench of stale cigarettes from his locker assaults me.

"Eww. Get off, Fido." He jabs an elbow, forcing me off him, and I stumble backward with a dull pain in my belly. His breath smells worse than his locker. If it weren't for his mom being the town shrink, he wouldn't be as popular as he is. Money isn't the only thing that talks in this town. He's everyone's main source of pills and a total asshat. He steals prescriptions right out from under his mom's nose!

As you can tell, I'm not one of those who count. If not for my mom being the chief of police, maybe things would be different. Maybe then I wouldn't be known as Fido, like some stupid K-9 dog. But I'm not a snitch. It's not my fault these idiots party in plain sight. What hurts is Shin thinks the same thing about me. That I told on him. I wouldn't do that. I was planning on talking to him with our best friend, Nora, about his drug problem, but she was gone. Mom somehow found out about it before Nora got back. Plus, Shin should've known better than to think it was me. Mom doesn't even stay in the same room with either of us long enough to tell her shit.

I hitch my bag further onto my shoulder as I step out of the school building, staring at the gymnasium across the courtyard. Since our school was built before—I don't know—sports, the gymnasium sits behind the school as a single building. Not that it's new or anything. It has the same old stench as the rest of the school.

Ugh. The band is already playing. I look to my right, at the student parking lot. Would anyone even notice if I left? Probably not, but I can't risk Mom finding out. Even if they are releasing us in thirty minutes. It isn't worth it. I cut my gaze back to the gym, squinting at the large bulldog painted on the bricks, and it looks just how I feel. Pissed off. I start across the courtyard as more students barrel out of the main building. A few bump into me, yelling and jumping on each other like clowns in a circus. They don't even acknowledge me or apologize.

I hate football season.

As I enter the gymnasium, the noise hits me all at once. Sneakers squeaking on the gym floor. Laughter or calling of friends. Shrills of girls gossiping about the golden boy or his stupid friends. The sharp sound of trumpets and drums. The mascot barking, and yes, it's an actual bulldog. It belongs to the coach's wife. Her prized possession, to be exact. And the smell, oh my god, it's overpowering. The stink of sweat from gym class five minutes ago is now mixed with all that perfume and cologne. I hate it.

I plug my ears as I hurry for the bleachers, weaving between a cluster of students. At the top, I take my usual spot and stare at the gym doors, searching for my best friend. *Where is she?* Normally, Nora is here first. I shove my backpack between my knees and clutch the top loop tightly as two students stomp by. They drop next to me, cheering and shoving each other. I feel like I'm suffocating. It's too hot. I can't breathe. I wipe sweat off my upper lip and then blow out a steady breath.

A whistle slices through the noise as the cheerleaders jog onto the polished floor, where another large bulldog is painted. They shake their gold and green poms at the crowd. Of course, the head cheerleader does somersaults, flipping across the gym. No one else is allowed to outshine her, and everyone here knows it. If I am lucky, she'll keep on flipping right out the gym doors and straight out of town. She stops in front of the other cheerleaders and raises one pom and knee at the same time. No such luck.

"Go Bulldogs!" she shouts through blood-red painted lips. They're probably that color because she's taken a bite out of some poor freshman on her way to—what she would call—her stage. She gracefully goes up onto another cheerleader's shoulders, shouting again.

Heather might not be the worst person in the world, but she's certainly the worst person in Canyon Falls. And her BFF standing directly behind her, ready to catch her, is worse than she is. Mark Ortiz is tall and wiry and claims everyone drains him mentally, but still seems to end up in the middle of everyone's shit. Mostly mine. I don't just hate Heather and Mark. I loathe them. And not because they are the ones who gave me my nickname, but for how they betrayed my brother.

A vibration rumbles under my feet as everyone stomps and cheers, and I can literally see Heather's head grow bigger. If that's possible. I reach into my bag for my phone and still nothing from Nora. I grip the pink sparkle case tightly in my lap, focusing on the doors. *Come on, Nora. Hurry.* My knee bounces.

After Heather does her solo cheer, the football coach clears his throat into the mic before introducing his star players. I roll my eyes. We know exactly who they are. We all grew up together. We even know each other's secrets. If by some small chance you do have a secret tucked away in your pocket, it won't be long before the secret is screamed down the hall like a fire alarm. Everyone will have heard it by lunch. And Heather's secret . . . well, those boobs didn't just grow over the summer, and Mark's nose . . . still has that brand new shine. And that's just this summer. The two of them have had nip and tuck parties for the last two years.

"Asher West."

Here comes the biggest douche-nozzle on the team. He's not just loud and obnoxious; he's dominating. Basically, the typical jock. He doesn't really have a secret. It's more like everyone forgot what a weirdo he was in grade school. Every time he touched something, a table, a book, or even another student, he would smell the tips of his fingers with this intense focus. It wasn't just weird, it leaned heavily on the creepy side.

But I'm the freak of the school because I follow the rules. *Got it.*

"Kingston Erikson."

Now, he's someone you wouldn't think is a jock with his tall, skinny physique and the way he dresses. I swear he looks like he just stepped out of the fifties. He even has the rizz to go with it. The kind of undeniable charm that pulls you in. Lucky for him, he didn't grow up in Canyon Falls. He moved here to live with his grandpa last year, so whatever secrets he has, no one knows them. *Yet.* But there are rumors about his parents circulating. Not vicious. More curious, like, where are they? What happened to them? Are they dead?

He jogs across the gym, and everyone goes crazy. I can practically feel the electricity he brings, and I don't blame them. He does have striking features. Square jaw. A contagious smile. Dreamy, sad brown eyes you could get lost in. And when he speaks, which isn't often, his voice is low and his words come out slow and deep. Okay, maybe I'm a little drawn to him, too, but I'd never act on it. Not when I have bigger problems to worry about.

"Ethan Bains." I glance at the double doors and when I don't see Nora, I clap and cheer for him.

When Shin was here, Ethan was a part of our group. The four of us—Nora, me, Ethan, and Shin—were practically glued together until last year. Then everything went to shit. Shin was caught with drugs. Mom freaked and immediately sent him off to live with Dad. Like, not even a conversation. Just called Dad and told him to come get Shin, and he was gone two days later. And Ethan, well, without Shin he needed to make his own way. Which meant guy friends. He did, but at the cost of Nora's reputation and friendship. At least that's what Nora says happened, but I don't see it. Ethan is a Sikh and one of the nicest people I know. His whole culture is about peace and kindness. He would never intentionally hurt Nora, or anyone for that matter. But for Nora, I pretend to be mad at him too.

My phone vibrates, and I turn it over. *Finally.*

NORA

Sorry, got caught in the office. OMW.
5 min.

My fingers tremble across the phone as I reply.

AMY

It's okay. I managed. It's about over anyway. Meet you in the courtyard?

NORA

Yeppers peppers!

A grin softens my breathing as I slide my phone back into my bag. After the coach gives the same speech he always gives, and the cheerleaders belt out another cheer, we are finally released for the day. I push to my feet, sling my backpack over my shoulder, and start down the bleachers. Determined to get out of here and quiet the noise, I force myself through the crowd, but I don't make it very far.

"Amy!" calls Theo, a sophomore and the kicker of the football team. He fights his way through with his hand raised. He's one of the very few people that isn't an asshat to me, and that alone makes me stop.

I meet him in the middle of the gym floor, and he looks around like he's afraid someone will see him talking to me. That's a first. Sweat forms in my armpits. I really hope he isn't going to try to make a name for himself by making fun of me. I grip the strap of my backpack tighter.

Theo turns back to me with a nervous smile, shoving his hands into his back pockets. "Do you think you could help me with my English paper?"

"I'm not writing your paper for you." I turn, and he swiftly slides in front of me.

"I didn't ask you to. See, I have Mrs. Ryan this year, and I thought since you had her last year, you would know what she likes and doesn't like, that kind of thing."

"It's English, Theo. It's pretty much the same as you had last year, just harder. Do your homework, and you'll be fine." I step around him, and he plants himself in front of me again.

"I seriously need a tutor." His green eyes dart from me to the other football players. "If I don't bring up my grades, Coach is going to kick me off the team." He runs a hand through his thick honey-blond hair and then looks at me with a lopsided grin. "I'll pay."

Now he has my attention. If I want to help Nora more than I already am, this will help immensely.

"How much?"

"I don't know." He shrugs. "I've never had a tutor before."

"Okay. How about $20 an hour?" I shift on my feet, scanning the gym, and it's nearly empty now. Only the star football players are left, and they're throwing a ball around.

I'm caught in Kingston's stare. He tosses the ball back to Asher and then lifts his chin at me with that boyish smile. My cheeks burn all the way to my toes. For a moment, as he stares at me, I forget I'm the school freak, and then I blink and the spell between us is gone. He's back to tossing the ball and joking with Asher.

"I can do that. When do you want to meet?"

I force my attention back to Theo. "Tomorrow? I can come over after dinner. Around seven," I say and step around him.

"You're a lifesaver, Amy!"

As I join everyone crowded outside, most are milling around, talking. And a few groups are slowly headed toward the student parking lot. I lift onto my toes, searching over bobbing heads for Nora. *Hurry! I want to go home.*

"Hey, Fido!"

My muscles tense at the whiny voice. I step around a group of guys, and one of them backs up, shoving me against the wall.

"Didn't you hear me calling you?" Mark corners me, smiling.

I twist my bag around, hugging it as I shuffle left, trying to escape.

"Where are you going?" Mark's grin widens as he lifts his phone, aiming it right at me. "Heather and I wanted to ask you a question."

Heather leaps, landing directly in my path with her black pigtails swinging behind her like two black cobras warming up to strike out.

"What do you want?" I ask, squeezing my bag tighter.

"Is it true dogs can't look up or they'll suffocate?" Mark nudges Heather.

"What?" I look to my right for another way out. Or better, Nora. My eyes light up. There she is. She's talking to Trisha.

"O.M.G. Do you have a thing for Robby?"

The second Heather asks, I see him in my line of sight. *Eww. Vomit my face off!* I face Heather. *That's mortifying. I really hope no one believes that.* "No," I mutter through clenched teeth.

"Good. You'd have a better chance at the dog park than with me," Robby says loudly.

I grind my teeth, clutching my bag so hard that my fingers hurt. It's moments like these when I wish Mom wasn't a cop.

"You know she can't understand you, Robby."

I cut my eyes to Heather's voice with heat fuming off of me. Her eyes narrow as she pulls a sucker out of her mouth, pointing the green tip at me. I can't tell if she's smiling or snarling. She really needs to cool it with the lip injections.

"Yeah, you have to speak her language, duh." And Heather and Mark both bark right in my face.

Humiliation burns my skin as I wipe the spittle off my cheek, wanting to smack the shit out of both of them. Hell, they're even lined up for me. Just one quick slap and I'd hit them both. But I can't be caught fighting. I have to follow the rules. Or Mom will send me off to live with Dad, just like Shin. Apparently, Mom's career and reputation mean more to her than her own children. And then what will become of Nora? I can't leave her here, alone. Not when she needs me the most.

Before Heather can bark a second time, Nora strides up with a scowl. She steps between us, and with her tall height, her wild red hair protects me like a copper shield. Nora is the only one who doesn't take their shit. Out of everyone in the school, I think Nora is the only one they are afraid of. With good reason. Nora has popped them both a few times. Since then, they usually only tease me, or anyone for that matter, when she isn't around. Nora hates bullies.

They both take a wide step back as curious eyes draw closer. Now it's my turn to smirk at the power shift.

"You know, for two people that friggin' talk so much, I'd think one of you would say something intelligent for once." Nora pauses a moment, eyeing them, and then reaches up. "And grow up. You're not twelve anymore." Without waiting for a response, Nora tugs the green and gold ribbon from one of Heather's pigtails, yanking a handful of her hair with it.

"Ow. What the fuck, Lurch?" Heather recoils, rubbing at her scalp as Mark snickers, but Nora doesn't linger to watch the fallout. She grabs my arm and leads me back toward the school with a confidence I wish I had. Even with everything Nora is going through, she still has a firm belief in herself. Who she is and what she wants out of this world and life.

"Nora," I begin, hooking my arm with hers. "You just had pigtails yesterday."

"I know." She grins. "But she's such a number two."

The way she calls someone an asshole always makes me chuckle.

"Plus." Nora emphasizes with a dramatic stiff finger nearly jabbing me in the face. "She nearly yanked out all of Beth's hair yesterday. Eye for an eye, right?"

"Yeah," I mutter, glancing over my shoulder. Heather is still glaring. Her flushed cheeks are a reddish-brown. I can't tell if it's out of embarrassment or anger as the court-yard breaks off into laughter. A chill runs down my back. I'm going to pay for this. I just know it.

I turn back, wondering what my brother would do if he knew his ex was bullying me. Probably nothing. He didn't do anything when he was dating Mark, but it has gotten worse since Shin moved. Plus, my brother is just as scared of messing up as I am now. If Mom had a different job, I'd be able to stand up for myself, instead of always relying on Nora to fight my battles.

But would I? I don't even have the nerve to stand up to my mom.

"Stop letting them get to you. They aren't worth it." Nora stops abruptly at the door and faces me. "Plus, we have bigger things to focus on. I'm working at his place today, so keep your phone on you. I don't wanna get knappered."

"Okay." I twist my bag around, digging through it for my phone. "Where are you going now? Want to come over before your shift starts?" I peek up at her, hoping she will, but Nora hasn't been over in months. Not since Mom told me I couldn't hang out with her anymore. "Mom's working, so it's safe. It'll give us time to work on the podcast."

"Dang, I really wish I could, but I already told Mr. Gibson we had a half day." Nora's face falls as she shifts on her feet. "He'll be waiting for me to clock in and start working. And I have to go home, change, and grab something to eat first." She starts to turn, and I can tell she's reluctant to leave me. She usually is. "But I'll check in before and after work."

"You better." I smile.

As Nora heads off, I watch her blend in with the crowd of students until she disappears. Guilt gnaws in my stomach. If she gets caught, we're both in trouble. As much as I miss Shin, I really don't want to go live with Dad. His rules are a lot worse than Mom's.

CHAPTER TWO
2:39 P.M.

NORA

The sun's harsh rays bounce off the water as I glide the pool net across its surface, catching leaves and loose grass. I pause for a moment, balancing the pole against my shoulder as I reach into the pocket of my overalls. I pull out a stick of cinnamon-flavored gum, remembering how days like this used to stretch into the next, like summer would never end. When we'd all meet over here for a game of hide and seek. Tag. Water volleyball. And at night, the twinkly lights strung across the pergola gave off just enough light for overnight campouts and late-night swimming.

But that was before Amy's parents divorced, and everything slowly changed between our group.

I dip the net back into the water, and every step I take along the pool reminds me that nothing here belongs to Amy and Shin anymore. Even when the house was empty for a couple of years, we still came here. Our secrets and confessions remained. It still belonged to us. But now, it belongs to the dude who lives here.

A puffy cloud blocks the heat for a moment, and a cool breeze sweeps over my shoulders. I step onto the lawn, shaking the last of the grass blades out of the net, tossing it back onto the freshly cut yard. After hanging the net against the rebuilt pool shed, I walk closer to the house, where my work cart is parked. Not only has he replaced everything, from the patio furniture, to the decking along the pool, to the pool slide, he's totally rebuilding the place. The back of the house, where the sun used to pour into Amy's room, is now walled up with red brick. There isn't even a single window back here, just a solid wooden back door. It used to be a sliding glass door.

The once pale-yellow siding, where paint chipped off in flakes from too much water and rain splattering on it, is now a stark white with black shutters added to the front of the house. And the gnarled tree that used to have a sturdy tree-house sitting at the top has been cut down, along with the tire swing and the jungle gym. It looks nothing like it used to. Like he's erasing everything about us. Our secrets, friend-ship, our childhood. So, you can understand why working for him has left a bad taste in my mouth. Hence, the friggin' gum.

Well, maybe not every memory. I don't have a clue what the inside looks like. I don't help when it comes to working indoors. That's the job of Mr. Gibson, my boss. He's the town handyman. Plumber. Electrician. Carpenter. He can do just about anything the client needs. Me, I'm the outside help. Cleaning pools. Fixing mailboxes. Painting the address on the curb. Mowing. A lot of friggin' mowing. And with Canyon Falls nearly off the grid, it's just easier for folks to call Mr. Gibson than to wait for a big company to come all the way out here. But since today is lawn and pool day, Mr. Gibson isn't here. It's just me.

I reach for the work bucket and then head to the pool, keeping an eye on the brown and black dog guarding the back door. Mr. Gibson says it's a Belgian-something and that it's friendly, but I've never gotten close enough to find out. It's super creepy the way it never moves from that spot, like it's chained, but it's not. It just lies on the back porch, watching my every move. I squat near the deep end with another glance at the dog. If I didn't know any better, with the house walled up so no one can see inside and a guard dog, I'd think this dude is trying to hide something. Not only is he super sketch, but he gives off some serious murdery vibes. Quiet. Keeps to himself. Old, maybe forty. Dark hair and eyes. Average height. Fit, but not muscular. You know—like a friggin' serial killer.

Normally, when someone new arrives, the entire town has the scoop on them by the end of the week. He's been here over a month, and he's still a complete mystery. Not even Amy's mom, the chief of police, knows anything about him. It's why Amy and I started our own investigation into him. We've even started a podcast about it. We call it *Root Down. How Well Do You Know Your Neighbors?* But before we can go live, we need more information about him. We've tried everything to get a glimpse inside the house, peering through slivers in the blinds. Looking through the garage window. We've even set up outside, right under the front bay window, listening for voices or screams. But the dude is like a ghost. We don't hear anything. Not even the TV or his dog. There are never any packages delivered. No visitors. And the mailbox is always empty.

I keep thinking if we could just get a quick look inside, without him here, maybe we'd find proof. But the dude is always home. It's like being detectives in one of those true crime shows, except the freak is right here in Canyon Falls, and we're the only ones who seem to care.

So, for now, we need to settle for watching and waiting and recording every suspicious detail for the podcast. And since I'm the one who works here, doing the mowing and crap, I have more access. And I've taken a crapload of pictures and videos. I'm waiting for him to make a mistake, and I'll have him.

I glance over at the dog. That's probably his partner in crime and the one that digs the graves. *Dang it! Why didn't I think of that before? Amy's going to flip.*

I pull my phone from the back pocket of my overalls, tap the screen, and then press record. I scan the row of newly built flower beds lining the back fence as I talk.

"Okay, new information. Mr. Stabby planted the corn-flowers last week. I didn't think anything about it then, but once I'm done with the pool, I'll check that for disturbed dirt." I turn the camera on myself. "If I find something, I'm going to freak." I stop recording, shove the phone back into my pocket, and return to work. I focus back on the lid leading to the main drain and reach inside for the skimmer basket. Combing my fingers along the sides, I rake out dead bugs and grass into the bucket next to me.

"Hey, kid, you about done?" His voice cuts through, sending my nerves into overdrive, hyperaware that I am alone with him.

My hand stops halfway inside the bucket. *How'd this*

mofo sneak up on me? I'm practically facing the house. I crane my neck, and he's watching me with a creepy, cold intensity, like he's sizing me up for a body bag. *Crap! Has he been out here this whole time? Watching me! Absolute psycho!*

My stomach drops. *Oh my God, did he hear and see everything I recorded?*

My heart races as I force on a smile. "Umm. Yeah," I squeak and then clear my throat, deepening my tone. "Just need to clean this out and shock it."

"Shock it?" He shifts, and I can't be certain if he's closer now. Pure adrenaline shoots straight into my veins.

I wet my lips, eyeing his boots, mentally marking his stance, and then lift my gaze. "Sorry, put some chlorine in it. But next week, you might want to start thinking about closing it down. Fall is right around the corner."

He tilts his head, pulling a long drag off his cigarette. *Ew. How did he get this close and I didn't smell that?*

"Okay," he says, blowing smoke. "I don't have time to stop by Gibson's today." He flicks the cigarette, and it lands five feet away from us, right into the sand bucket near the lounge chairs. *Gross. I'm not cleaning that out.* "So come on in when you're done and grab the new designs for the cabinets. Plus, there's something I'd like to discuss with you. It's important."

Umm. That's gonna be a hard no, Mr. Stabby. Ever since Mr. Gibson and I started working for this freak, he's been trying to talk to me. Probably so he can lure me into his dungeon. But I've seen *Silence of the Lambs.* No way am I getting knappered.

I cough into my fist and then point to my throat. "I think I'm coming down with something." Turning around,

I drop the skimmer back into the hole. "I should probably stay out here," I say, closing the lid with another fake cough.

"I'm not scared of a little cold," he says with a quick slap on the back of my shoulder, and I nearly pitch forward, right into the pool. My eyes bulge as I reposition myself. Okay, so he's a heck of a lot stronger than he looks. Which, I guess you'd have to be if you're lugging dead bodies around in the middle of the night.

With the most terrifying swallow, and hopefully not my last, I push to my feet and back away from him, nearly toppling over the diving board. "Yeah, well, you know, can't be too careful nowadays." I chuckle. At least I hope it sounded like a chuckle and not an actual scream of terror.

He shifts into a defensive stance, folding his arms over his chest with his brows pinched. *Doubly crap!* Mr. Stabby's staring at me like he can't decide if he wants to choke the life from me or drown me right here in the pool. I need to be careful. Play it cool. Just one wrong slip-up and I'll be his next victim.

I force a smile. "Welp." I nervously chuckle again and shoot him finger guns, making a clicking sound. "Gotta get back to work." I turn and jump over the diving board, hurrying to my work cart for the bags of shock.

Great. If he didn't think I was the perfect victim before, he definitely does now. I basically ran away from him like a scared little mouse. Threw out finger guns like a friggin' dork that has no friends. And on top of that, if he has been following me around, like killers do, he knows I'm practically raising myself. He could grab me, and no one would ever know.

I grab two bags of shock and then reach into the square chest pocket of my overalls, pulling out my box knife.

Okay, Amy would know, but by the time she told her mom, I'd be dead.

"Are you always this jumpy, kid?"

"Jesus." I clutch at my chest, inching away on wobbly knees. *Why is this sneaky mofo following me? Oh, that's right, he's going to murder me.*

His phone rings, and I gulp, inching closer to the side fence. I need to finish this job quickly.

"You should be careful with that. You're lucky the blade wasn't out." He points at the box knife close to my chest while pulling his cell phone out of his back pocket. The freak doesn't even say hello. He just puts the phone up to his ear, watching me walk over to the shallow end of the pool. If this mofo only says "I understand" and then hangs up, I'm friggin' outta here.

I slice the box blade along the corner of the bags and walk around the pool, slowly pouring in the shock. But also keeping my eye on him and his dog. I'm not letting either one sneak up on me. Not again, anyway. Next time I'm here, I need to be a lot more careful and aware of my surroundings.

"And you're sure about this?" He lifts his gaze to the sky and then back at me. "Kid, come here," he says, aggressively walking toward me. "I need you to come inside with me."

Nope. That's not happening. I'm outta here. I dump the rest of the shock into the pool, and the wind blows, hurling the shock back at me, forcing a violent cough out. I drop the bags and they float into the pool as I start for the side gate, trying to blink the fiery fumes of chlorine from my eyes. "Sorry, can't. I got another job," I say, hurrying my steps.

"I'm not asking. Get inside the house." He rounds the pool for me with his hand stretched out. "Nora!"

For a split second, I freeze at the command in his voice, and then I remember it's Mr. Stabby. Absolutely no friggin' way am I going anywhere with him. Especially in his house. Alone.

The dog lifts up, growling. I rush forward, slamming into the side gate. My hand fumbles for the latch, and I chance a look over my shoulder. He calls for me again, and I turn back, throw the latch over, and push, but the gate sticks, only opening slightly. Before he can grab me, I squeeze through, ripping the side pocket of my overalls clean off. *That will be the only piece of me you'll be getting, psycho!* I sprint across the lawn.

Hopping into Mr. Gibson's red beat-up truck with my heart nearly exploding, I pull away from the curb like a maniac. I peek into the rearview mirror, and thankfully he isn't chasing me. I squint back at the road with my eyes watering and turn down Greenwood Lane, taking the back way. With shaky hands, I pull over while staying hyper-aware of any car barreling down the road. I reach over for a bottle of water and dip my head back to flush out my eyes.

"Siri, FaceTime Amy."

CHAPTER THREE

2:46 P.M.

SHIN

I never should have left home the way I did. Full of anger and hurt, but it's too late to go groveling back now. Not that Dad would take me back after the things I said to him. But to threaten me with military school all because I started hanging around a crowd he didn't approve of is . . . just crazy.

My fingers tighten around the glass as I watch water swirl down the kitchen drain. And Mom, she probably doesn't even care that I ran off or where I might be. She's the one who threw me out. The one that didn't want me because I was "too much to handle."

I wish Grandpa was still alive. He was the only one who ever got me, and why I go by my middle name, Shin, now, instead of Eric. It's the only way I know how to honor him. What sucks, though, is it was the one and only time Mom was proud of me. But I didn't do it for her—although she'd like to take the credit—I did it for me and Grandpa and the bond we shared.

I dip the cup under the water and then drain the glass so fast that I gulp for air. I fill it back up and turn, leaning against the sink. Ethan walks into the kitchen, wearing his green jersey and a matching Dastar. Damn, I've missed him.

"We're all good. Dad is working late," he says, opening the refrigerator. "He won't be back until the game starts."

I step forward and rest against the marble island. "Are you sure it's okay if I stay here for a couple of days? I can't go home, not yet." I shift my weight as my stomach knots with worry. I've been on the move, trying to make my way here for two days, and I haven't really slept yet. Maybe a few hours on the bus. But now that I am here, I'm too scared I might run into someone I know. And Amy, well, I can't see her yet. Not until I make things right with Mom.

"It's all good." Ethan tosses a box of cold pizza onto the counter. "I'm just glad you're back. Even if it is only for a few days." Ethan ducks his head back into the refrigerator. "Have you spoken to Amy? Does she know you're in town? Or are you still freezing her out until you settle all this?"

"Yeah," I mutter, staring at the water glass, thumbing the cold, wet condensation.

After what Ethan said happened today at school, and all the other shit he's told me in the last year, guilt stabs my chest. Amy already takes so much shit from everyone; she shouldn't get it from me too. I wish things were different between us. I hate how everything turned out. How I had to leave. The friendships I left behind. But mostly, how I hurt Amy. Every time she texts or calls, my heart constricts because of the lies I've had to tell her or the one-word responses. Even through a text, I feel the disappointment and pain I've caused her.

"I get it." Ethan holds the handles of the refrigerator, looking over his shoulder. "Want soda, tea, or are you sticking with water?"

"Water is fine." I reach over, sliding the pizza box closer to me. "How is she? Amy. I mean when Heather and Mark aren't messing with her. Is she happy?"

"From the small conversations I've had with her, yeah, she seems happy." He pulls out a can of soda, kicking the door shut with his foot. "And even with Mark and Heather, it isn't too bad usually, with her watchdog protecting her."

I grin as I flip the pizza box open. "Nora has always been protective of her. All of us, actually. One of the reasons I knew she'd be okay without me." I grab a slice. "What about you and Nora? You said some shit happened between you two, but you never told me about it." I fold the pizza, taking a huge bite, watching him. "Are you going to tell me?" I ask with a mouthful.

"Honestly, I have no idea. She won't tell me what I did. One day we were tight, goofing around like we normally do, and the next she refused to speak to me." He braces his elbows on the counter. "I've even asked Amy, and she won't tell me either. She just says, 'You'll need to talk to Nora about it.'"

I roll the bite over to the side of my cheek, asking, "Is Amy giving you the cold shoulder too?"

"Only when Nora is around." He grins, then his dark brown eyes are a mix of sadness and anger. He straightens, popping the can open. "Then again, Nora hasn't been the same since her last trip into foster care."

I'm about to ask how long she was gone this time, but he continues.

"I mean, she was only gone for a couple of months this time. Everything was cool, too . . . for a hot minute. Then, out of nowhere, she stopped wearing makeup and doing her hair. It's either crazy wild like she hasn't brushed it in days, or it's pulled into a tight bun or braid. And every day, it's pretty much the same clothing. Jeans, flannel or tank top, depending on the time of year, and the same dirty white Vans that look brown now. I mean, she really let herself go, and not just with her appearance. Her attitude is either crappy or mean, depending on her mood, and her mood is usually hard to read. So, you never know what you're going to get until you approach her. And lately, she's been super paranoid. Reads into everything you say or do."

"Have you tried talking to her about it?" I eye him, knowing how he is. He's sort of spoiled, and when he doesn't get his way, he pouts. "I mean more than once."

"No." He fidgets with his steel bracelet. "Like I said, we aren't on speaking terms." He looks back at me, annoyed. "And even if we were, she reads into everything. Nora is not the girl you remember, Shin. Something happened to her . . . and Amy. They are both different, secretive."

Before I can ask follow-up questions, the back door crashes open, hitting the table and chairs wedged into a corner. I jerk straight up, nearly shitting myself and choking on my food, as Asher enters like the Kool-Aid guy.

He cups his mouth with a loud and obnoxious, "Party's here, mother—whoa." He stops just inside the door and cocks his head. "Shin?" His lips tug into a lopsided grin as he starts forward. "Bro, I barely recognized you. What are you doing here? Are you back?"

"I don't know." I shrug, reaching for the glass of water.

"God, I hope so. I've missed you." He walks around the kitchen island and clamps his hands onto my shoulders, squeezing. "Either way, it's good to see you."

"Hey, we still on for after the game?" He reaches over, slapping Ethan on the cheek. Not hard, just enough to irritate him. Ever since I've known Ethan, he has hated anyone touching his face. I don't blame him; he's worked really hard to clear up all the acne. He still has some, but it isn't as bad as it used to be.

"No. Shin doesn't want his mom to know he's back yet. So, we're going to come back here after the game and hang."

"So? It's not like the chief's invited." Asher reaches for a slice, shoving half of it into his mouth. "Trust me, it's out at Theo's farm. No one will call on us."

"Yeah, but everyone else will know, and you know how this town is." I reach over, grabbing another slice of pizza. "Secrets don't stay hidden long, especially about someone coming back."

"Bro, come on. It's the first party of the year. You gotta go. Especially if you're here to stay. It's a great way to make your mark for senior year." His voice rises with a hint of challenge.

"He's right. And if you are planning on talking to your mom, does it really matter?" Ethan agrees.

For a moment, I feel the pressure all over again. But this time it isn't the whole town eager to see what I'll do next. It's from Asher and Ethan. I clench my jaw, fighting the urge to fold, and that is something I can't do. I can't go back to the way I was, causing trouble for attention or popularity. I've seen how that goes. It isn't good. This time, I'm going to be more like Amy. Good.

"Yeah, maybe. I have to talk to my mom first. I have a lot of explaining and groveling to do. Then we'll see if she allows me to move back or not."

"She will. She has to. I'll even come help grovel." Ethan grins, pulling his phone out of his back pocket. "Crap. The coach wants us on the field, like now." He peers up at me. "Want us to drop you off at your house so you can talk to your mom, or are you staying here?"

"Neither, but you can give me a ride to the pharmacy. I need to refill my meds and pick up a few things." I try to sound casual, but my tone still comes out a little too heavy. Nervous. I straighten with my pulse racing. If I run into Mom before I'm ready, I might blow it. I might say something stupid again and the apology I have memorized may never be said. I could ruin everything before I have a chance to prove to her that I've changed. That I will change.

"Noice. Kingston is at the pharmacy," Asher says with a wide grin. "We can pick him up while we're there."

"Who?" I ask, rubbing my clammy hands down my jeans as I try and steady my breathing. I'm so nervous. I didn't know it would be this bad. Everything I envisioned on my way here, my speech and groveling, didn't have the emotions attached to it. But now that it's getting closer to actually talking to Mom, I might have a panic attack.

"That's right. You haven't met him. He moved here right after you left. His grandpa is Mr. Erikson." Asher reaches for the last slice. "He's our new quarterback and a legend. Bro has changed the game for all of us." Asher lifts the pizza like he's making a toast, grinning. "This year, we are going to take state." He winks and then starts for the back door. "You should see him on the field. He's the real deal, like scouts coming just for him." Asher stops at the door and faces me. "And I think he has a thing for your sister."

"He does?" I ask with surprise. From what Ethan says, Amy isn't well-liked. Now I want to meet this guy. There's something intriguing about someone who doesn't follow the crowd. I'd say like me, but honestly, I only caused trouble to fit in, to prove I didn't care who my mom was. But for someone to see Amy for more than just the rumors tugs at my curiosity.

"Well, he's not come out and said it, but everyone can tell," Ethan agrees, grabbing his bag by the door on his way out.

"Everyone but Amy." Asher turns, walking backward as I grab my bag and close the back door behind me. "Did you tell Shin how Kingston laid Robby out?"

"No. I didn't know he did. When did this happen?" Ethan asks as we walk down the long driveway to Asher's beat-up, rusted car parked on the curb.

Asher stops at the back end of his car with a wide grin, rubbing his hands together. "Check this, Kingston and I were in the gym, tossing the ball around, when Theo jogs up to us. He tells us what just happened out in the court-yard, and what Robby said about Amy. On how gross she is or something." Asher waves a dismissive hand, looking over at Ethan. "Anyway, Kingston grins at me. You know the look. The one he gets when he's about to mess someone up. Well, he tosses me the ball, walks straight out of the gym, and punches Robby. Boom." He throws an air punch and then bounces on his toes. "Bro, never even broke stride, just kept walking until he caught up with Amy." Asher jingles keys out of his pocket as he makes his way to the driver's side. "Best thing I've ever seen, bro."

"Really?" Ethan asks, opening the passenger door and lightly shaking his head. "I wish I could have seen that."

"Me too." I grin, pushing the front seat forward and squeezing into the back. "It sounds like Nora isn't Amy's only friend after all."

Asher settles into the driver's seat and then peers at me from the rearview mirror. "Have you seen her yet? Nora."

"No, but Ethan said she's changed and is a little distant." I pull my knees close as the seat slams back and Ethan slides into the front.

"*Changed* isn't the word I'd use." Asher whistles and pulls away from the curb. "More like she's transformed into a completely different person."

"I told you," Ethan says, twisting in his seat to look at me. "She's right on the edge of crazy."

"Yeah, but in a hot way." Asher winks at me, then focuses on the road.

"Eww." Ethan's nostrils flare as his nose scrunches. "Are you serious?"

"Yeah, she's all legs." Asher turns out of the neighborhood and onto Main Street.

I look out the window, ignoring them arguing over Nora, and I stare down the road that leads to Nora's place. The trailer park sits at the edge of the woods. I wonder if she'll be there tonight. I'd like to see her again. Out of the four of us, Nora was the one I enjoyed being around the most. No matter what was going on in her life, she was always there for me. She'd stop everything just to sit and listen to me bitch. Never judging or laying blame, even when I was at fault.

I face forward, wondering where she is. If it's possible to see her. Would she want to see me after freezing Amy out? Probably not.

We stop at the only stop sign in town, and I can literally see the town square up ahead. Where all the businesses are located. If we walked, we'd probably make it there faster. We're only a hop, skip, and a jump away. I look to my left, where kids are playing on the only jungle gym in town. In fact, it's part of our school. Pre-K–12. I mean, if you stood at the end of the Pre-K hallway and threw a football down it, it would land at a senior's feet.

Asher pulls forward, and I watch the green and gold banner hanging above the school's entrance. The wind catches it, and it sags further. It no longer says *Go Bulldogs!* All I can see now is *Go.* How I wish that were true. But I don't have anywhere else to go. I just hope Mom will actually listen to me this time. But what I want most is for Amy to forgive me. I only wanted to protect her.

CHAPTER FOUR
2:59 P.M.

AMY

Normally, I'm all about Nora's paranoia, but not today. Right now, she's freaking out more than usual. I feel awful. I should have known better than to push her into investigating Mr. Stabby. Nora has major trust issues, but I honestly never thought it would go this far. Plus, I thought it would give her something else to focus on instead of what's really happening in her home life.

I cut my eyes to my laptop, staring at the video I was editing from last week's investigation. Now I feel like a complete ass. I should have told her everything I found out about him weeks ago. Like how he's supposed to join the police force once his family joins him. And his dog is like his partner or something. Or it was his partner in the military. I can't remember. But Nora's paranoia and the scenarios she conjures in her head until she's in a frenzy are what make a good podcast. The perfect mystery of Flynt James.

"I swear, Ams, Mr. Stabby was about to murder me. Like for real." Nora's voice trembles on the edge of panic. Her flushed face intensifies each freckle, and her brown eyes, usually playful and promising loyalty, are now heavy and bloodshot.

"I'm so sorry, Nora." I shift, leaning back into the bar stool, and the wood groans. It's almost as if it's in tune with my emotions.

"It's fine." She blows her nose, and guilt stabs through my chest.

It's not fine. I've pushed her too far.

She's been crying.

"I'm about to go to the square. Mr. Gibson is working at the theater, and hopefully I can get to him before Mr. Stabby and save my job." She chews on her thumbnail. Her nervous habit, but when she keeps looking behind her, I can tell she's really scared, too, and not just about losing her job. Whatever really happened, Flynt James has gotten under her skin.

"Me too. I hate that this happened." I pick at the chipped crack along the kitchen bar with concern pounding against my chest. I feel so awful adding this fear onto her. It's time to tell her the truth. "Hey, there's something I need to tell you, but you can't get—"

"Whoa." Nora cranes her neck, looking out the windshield. "Are you looking outside, Ams?"

"No. Why?"

"It looks like a storm is coming. It's getting dark outside, but I don't see any clouds. Freaky. Only a small black dot like it's about to block out the sun. What do you think it could be? An eclipse?"

I glance to my left, at the bay window. She's right. The

sky is darker, but it's probably just a storm. Nine times out of ten, Nora's imagination takes over, and normally I'd say something about it. But with her already upset about Flynt, I don't want to add fuel to the fire. I face the phone, and she lifts a hand, squinting my way.

"If it is an eclipse, I hope I didn't do any damage."

"Me neither." My brows pinch. "Why did you even look at it, goofball?"

Her eyes widen as she throws a hand out dramatically. "Well, I didn't know it was an eclipse until I looked."

A small smile creeps in. "Can you see?"

She blinks rapidly. "Yeah, I can see. They're a little dry though, but that might be from the chlorine."

"The what? How did you manage . . . " The front door slams shut with my mom calling for me. "Ugh. Mom is home, and she sounds pissed. Call me back after you talk to Mr. Gibson."

Nora looks out the windshield again, distracted. "Yeppers peppers," she mutters.

I lower the phone and lean to my right, peering out the kitchen door. Mom is striding down the hall, quick and efficient, like I'm in big trouble.

Shit. Did Mom find out about Nora?

A rush of panic hits me as I slump over the laptop. I scroll the pad, pretending to shop for shoes with my hands trembling. Nora's secret, and the fact that I'm still friends with Nora, are the only two secrets I've kept from Mom. Okay, three if you count spying on Flynt James. Oh, and the podcast. So, I have more than a few secrets. Who doesn't? But Mom crossed the line when she forbade me from hanging out with Nora.

Ever since Shin got into trouble with drugs, Mom

thinks it's only a matter of time before Nora turns into a drug addict like her mom. Deep down, I truly believe Mom thinks Shin turned to drugs because he was friends with Nora. She hasn't come out and said that, but it's there. I can see it in her face every time Nora's name is mentioned. I guess forbidding me from hanging out with Nora is her way of saving the good child. As if she can't see the shit-storm she's created in her own home. Why else would Shin turn to drugs? It's not because of Nora. She follows all the rules. Worse than me. She doesn't drink or party. Hell, she doesn't even swear. Nora is such a goody-two-shoes; she's even given herself a curfew. If Mom spent more than a few minutes with her, she would know that, but then Mom would need to be in the same room as me.

If Mom finds out I haven't stayed away from Nora, and I also gave her my old phone to use, Mom might send me away too. Just the thought of never seeing Nora again makes my stomach hurt. So, I'm really hoping this is about something else. I mean, she doesn't even do the bills anymore. It's all automated. Part of why I thought I could get away with giving Nora the phone. Even if Mom actu-ally took the time to look at the bills, I can always lie and say I forgot to send it back. But if she finds out I've been friends with her this whole time, I'm finished.

"Amy, come with me." Mom grabs for my arm, and I pull out of her reach. Mom's face is tight with worry, and her high-bun is now hanging low on the back of her head.

My heart pounds so hard against my chest, my body feels like it's on fire. "Why?" I ask. This has to be about the phone bill.

"Because I said so." My heart drops. Still, I remain seated. "For once, Amy, do as I say." Her tone is mean and ugly. She sounds just like Dad. This time, when Mom grabs for me, she makes contact and yanks me to my feet. "Let's go," she says through her teeth.

"Okay. Dang." I reach for my phone and laptop as she practically drags me down the hallway, never breaking stride. My heart races even faster. "Mom, am I in a lot of trouble?"

She glances over her shoulder at me. She looks scared. "No, Amy, you aren't in trouble."

I have no idea why Mom is freaking out if she doesn't know about Nora. I haven't done anything else, unless she found out about us spying on Flynt.

My stomach knots as she pulls me into her office. She marches around the desk toward the bookcase. *Is she seriously about to put me in the corner? I thought I wasn't in trouble.*

She looks over her shoulder, like ten times, and then lifts a shaky hand for one of the books. Instead of pulling out a book, she tugs on the spine and pushes it back as if that's not the one she wants to give me, then she looks over her shoulder again.

Seriously? If I'm not in trouble, then what the hell is going on with Mom? Why is she acting so weird? And what stupid book is she about to give me to read? As if I need more reading material. It's bad enough between her and Dad that I have a stack of them in my room.

I release a bored sigh. Gears move, grinding behind the bookcase. I take an uneasy step backward as the bookcase slides along tracks, revealing a hidden door. *What the hell?*

Mom glances over her shoulder before stepping forward to punch in a code.

"Mom, is this some kind of secret room?" I scan

Mom's office. I've been in here a hundred times, even walked past this bookcase, totally clueless there was a hidden room here.

Nora is going to lose her shit when I tell her about this.

"It's a safe room." Mom opens the secret door.

"When did we get a safe room?" I ask. *Someone has binged* Panic Room *too many times.*

"It came with the house." Mom tugs on her earlobe. A tell I learned last year.

I squint at the lie. *Why lie about a stupid room?*

Mom clears her throat and sniffs. Another tell that she's holding something back. "I have to go to the station, but I won't be long. There are clothes in the black bag. Bottom shelf. Get dressed." Mom grabs my arm, her voice trembling as she practically shoves me inside the room. I stumble forward, catching myself on the metal shelf lined with supplies. When I turn, Mom's wide eyes are frantic. Her breath hitching. "Stay in here until I get back. Don't open the door or leave, no matter what you hear. Got it?"

"Mom . . . " I step forward, and she shuts the door in my face. *Really?*

I turn, staring at the bag Mom pointed at, and kick it. Hard. I don't want to be locked in this stupid room. And I'm definitely not wearing whatever crap is in that bag. My comfy boot shorts and matching tank top is fine. It's not like I'm leaving the house.

Movement catches my eye, and I whip my head to the left. I squint at the four security screens and march over to them. This is exactly how Shin was caught. I fumble with my laptop as I snap a photo. Wait until I prove to Shin that it wasn't me who told on him. Mom knew it, too, and she still forced Shin to leave, knowing he would blame and hate me.

A shiver of mistrust and anger twists in my gut. *Bitch move, Mom.*

After roughly pushing her keyboard and mouse and all her other shit onto the floor, I put my laptop in their place. Good thing I've never done anything in the house that would out me. Or Nora. I can't believe Mom has gone this far. With one last look at the screens, I drop into the chair and text Nora. I type fast and angrily as I go off about Mom's latest shit, but then I hesitate with my thumb hovering over the send. *What if Mom is watching every-thing, including my messages?*

Paranoia creeps in. I delete it all and just go with:

AMY

Hey, you aren't going to believe where I am

I wait for a reply, and regret drops in my belly as I scan the small room. It's so clean and sterile. Everything is in its place with military perfection. I lower my gaze to the mess I created, and my knee bounces with panic as her words stab at me. *"For once, Amy, do as I say."*

As if I haven't been doing that for ten years.

I glance at the phone. No message.

AMY

Grr. I'm in a safe room!

I put the phone down, chewing on my lip, tearing at the dry skin until I taste blood. *Screw this. I'm not staying locked in here until I know what's going on.*

I lift out of the chair and open the safe room door, but the second I step out, a loud pop and sizzle fills the room. The electricity goes out.

Shit! Now I'm finished.

CHAPTER FIVE

3:05 P.M.

NORA

At the stop sign, I slowly tap the brake pedal, and a cold breeze sweeps in the open window. A shiver ripples down my back. Maybe I should go home and grab a jacket. The temperature has really dropped. I tap a finger on the steering wheel, debating, when a sharp horn blares behind me. In the rearview mirror, a car speeds toward me.

Crap! Is that Mr. Stabby? No way am I going home now.

I jerk the wheel right with my eyes glued to the rearview. The car blows through the stop sign, bouncing at the dip in the road, headed straight.

Get it together, Nora. It wasn't even a black car.

I look forward, lifting my foot slightly off the gas pedal with another glance behind me.

If he hasn't come after you already, he isn't. Or is he waiting until dark? Crap. Maybe I shouldn't go home tonight.

I stop again, and another car drives right through the

stop sign. *And Amy says I'm a bad driver.* I turn right onto Main Street, where most of the major shops are, with a quick glance at the sky. If that is an eclipse, it's barely even over the sun. Plus, it's not done any damage to my eyes. Isn't that like part of an eclipse, not looking at it? I have three times now.

Looking back at the road, I instantly grip the steering wheel tighter, slamming on the brakes. The tires screech against the asphalt, and I come to a skidding halt, inches from hitting a linebacker.

Holy crap! Talk about a moron. Asher West gets on my friggin' nerves to the point I want to scream. Every other word out of him is *bro this* or *bruh that.* I hate it. But that's not the only reason I avoid him. He still doesn't understand what pansexual means. The idiot actually thinks Amy's brother has a thing for pots and pans. Sometimes you just can't talk to stupid. I honestly don't know how Shin and Ethan are friends with him.

Ethan steps out between two cars, joining Asher, and my heart skips a beat. Then my face falls as I force myself to stop smiling. Ever since I came back from foster care last year, I've been giving Ethan the silent treatment or starting arguments over small stuff. Just so he won't find out what happened, because out of Amy, Shin, and him, Ethan is the one that would tell an adult. But sometimes when I see him, I forget why I can't be friends with him. It hurts like heck, too, to treat him this way, but I can't afford for him to know the truth about me. It was hard enough telling Amy, but not telling her is like not breathing. I don't know what I would do without her. She is the only person I fully trust.

Asher hits the top of the hood. "Bro, we're walking here."

I lean out the window, hollering, "Yeah, and I don't see a crosswalk. Now move, bruhhh!"

They jog out of the way. Of course, Asher flips me off as he stands smack-dab in the only open parking spot on the square. *Really!* Before I can lay on the horn, Shin comes out of nowhere and pulls Asher onto the curb.

Holy cannoli! When did he get back into town? Last I heard, he swore he'd never return. I wonder if Amy knows he's back. Or if she knows what he looks like now. I mean, Shin has always been seen as the bad boy by all our parents, but super popular in school. He didn't have just one clique. He belonged to all of them. He got high with the burnouts. Played ball with the jocks. And was in all the clubs with the brains. Shin Mori was friends with everyone. Even the loners and rejects follow him. But now, he actually looks the part.

The dude is wearing half a kilt trailing behind ripped black jeans. Some sort of fancy white shirt with a purple tie that matches the hues in the kilt. A black leather jacket that fits perfectly with his skinny frame. He's definitely not the chubby Shin I remember. And his once-short hair is now long and bleached a stark white, with a slouchy beanie pulled low. On top of all that, he has a piercing dead center of his bottom lip. *Shin Mori got friggin' hot! I hope he's here to stay.*

Creeping into the parking spot, I'm careful to not hit the curb because, let's face it, Amy's right. I'm a terrible driver. I don't even have a license. Thankfully, Mr. Gibson doesn't know. He pays me in cash every week. Otherwise, he wouldn't let me drive his truck, and I probably wouldn't have this job. I don't have any information you need for tax stuff. I don't even know where my birth certificate is or what my social security number is.

I jam the gear in park and turn the key. *Play it cool, Nora.* I try to jump out of the truck, but I forgot I had the seatbelt on, and it nearly slingshots me back inside. My entire face burns as I unclick it, then slide out of the truck. Shin stops in front of me, smiling. *Don't say anything stupid.*

"Hey, Nora, what's good?"

Before I realize Shin is coming in for a hug, I lift my fist. "You know the vibes. Dab me up."

Oh my god! Why did I say that? Put your fist down, moron.

"Okay." He chuckles deep, slowly bumping his fist against mine.

Why didn't I hug him? I'm such a dork. Humiliation burns all the way to my toes. I have to get out of here before I embarrass myself further. Plus, I need to ask Amy if she knows he's back and what he looks like now.

"Welp, check ya later." I start to shoot him with finger guns, then catch myself. Instead, I brush by him with my body straight as a board, onto the curb.

"Yeah, maybe."

When I hear the hurt in Shin's voice, I turn back to apologize, but he's already talking to Ethan. Who, by the way, is pulling him down to the corner toward the pharmacy. Far away from me. Probably blaming me for the reason we aren't friends anymore. Which it is, but still.

"Smooth, bro?" Asher says, chewing on his stupid mouth guard.

"Shut up," I say through my teeth and then start down the sidewalk toward the theater.

Geez. Now, the whole town is going to hear about how I made a fool out of myself over Shin. Crap. I need to tell Amy about this first. Before she hears some exaggerated version from Asher and thinks I'm making a move on her brother.

I go for my phone and realize I left it in the truck. *Crap.* I turn and then remember why I'm here. I need to get to Mr. Gibson before Mr. Stabby does. One problem at a time. Mr. Gibson, then Amy. Instead of heading back to the truck, I walk to the theater.

CHAPTER SIX

3:10 P.M.

SHIN

My chest clenches at Nora's reaction. She squeezed by me as if she were afraid I'd touch her and then ran off. I guess it's a good thing I called Ethan when I got into town instead of her. She seems to blame me for icing out Amy. I don't blame her. With her mom in and out of rehab, I understand her not wanting to deal with someone else on drugs. I just wish things were different. That I could turn back time and stop everything bad from happening.

Ethan tugs on my shoulder, and I follow him and Asher down the sidewalk. We stop in front of Canyon Falls Pharmacy, and I glance one last time at Nora. She stops in front of the theater, then looks my way. We lock eyes, and, for a moment, I think she smiles. My heart jumps. Maybe I misread the whole thing. I really need my friends now more than ever. I start toward her, and Asher steps into my path. I glance over his shoulder, but she's already gone. *Shit! Maybe I can catch her later.*

A freezing cold breeze whistles through the town square. I pull my jacket closer.

"Bro, you feel that?" Asher mutters, looking skyward and rubbing his arms.

"Yeah." I follow his gaze.

Directly above us, black and purple clouds roll and churn at a fast rate. *Where did those come from? It was sunny seconds ago.* The town silences, and I lower my eyes, scanning Main Street. People on the street are glancing at their phones, pulling their children closer, and then the slow sound of a tornado siren screams in the distance.

I nearly jump out of my skin at the bell chiming to my right. I turn, and a preppy kid is standing in front of the pharmacy, holding the door open. "Whoa. Tonight's game is going to be epic with that storm."

He turns his head slightly, and my jaw tightens. Shaved on the left side of his head is his football number. 23. My number.

"Kingston, get inside here." Mr. Erikson yanks his grandson back inside the shop. Then he looks at Ethan and Asher. "Go home, and run." He eyes me, like he wants to say something. Instead, he says, "You, too, Shin." He closes the door, locks it, and then pulls a shade down.

"That was weird. It's just a tornado," Ethan says.

"Yeah, I guess Kingston doesn't need a ride after all."

Ethan looks up, muttering, "We should get to the field." He drops his gaze to mine. "Will you be okay on your own?"

"Of course," I laugh. "I'm not a child." But deep inside, I feel like one. A lost one at that.

"All right, see ya later."

"Yep."

A longing to fit in, to be wanted by someone, anyone, thickens my throat as I jog across the street. I duck into the alley, then lean against the Twisted Heads salon. I pull out my phone, staring at the screen with my thumb hovering over Mom's number. If I call her, she might agree with Dad and send me off. I don't want to be shipped off, but I also don't know what else to do. I'm about to hit the call button and hear a police siren in the distance. I glance down the street, and a cop car is speeding my way with its lights on. *Well, that didn't take long.* Mr. Erikson probably called my mom and told her I was in town.

A mix of emotions thunder in my chest as I step off the curb. I dry a sweaty palm down my jeans, walking between two cars. As I stop near the intersection, my heart races. Even if it isn't Mom, her sending a car this fast makes me wonder if I had her pegged wrong.

The closer the car gets, the more my throat closes. The apology I've been working on for the past two days runs through my head. I rehearse it again so I get it right.

I bounce on my toes, and when it's a few feet from me, I lift a hand. It is Mom. My throat closes completely as I fight back tears.

She doesn't stop.

She speeds by, rounding the next street.

She didn't even look my way.

I drop my hand, squeezing it into a fist as I move back onto the sidewalk. I guess I did have her pegged right after all. She wasn't even looking for me.

I draw in slow, controlled breaths as I sidestep deeper into the shadows of the alley. Instead of punching the red bricks that form the beauty salon, I lean against them. I hate her. And myself for thinking she cared. When will I learn?

I glance down Main Street at the theater. I need to talk to Nora. Even if she's pissed at me, she won't turn me away. She'll make time for me. Sit with me. Nora will listen.

I push off the bricks, and my phone blares in warning.

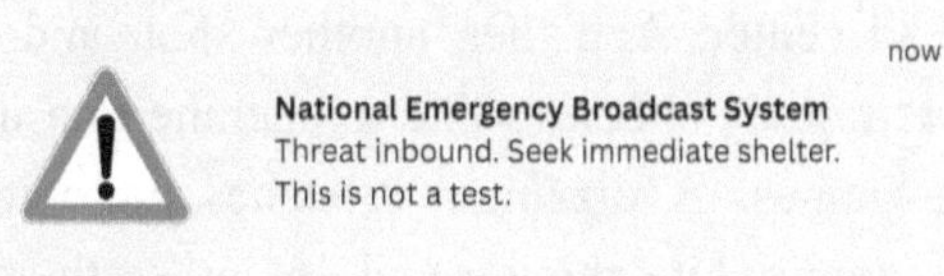

The salon door opens with women rushing out of it. I peek around the corner. They still have curlers and foil in their hair.

"Shin?" I step fully out, and Mrs. Mandy, the owner of the salon, adds, "Why are you just standing there? Get home." Her eyes flick up, and her face turns as white as her hair. She takes off down the sidewalk.

Wherever the tornado is forming, it's about to touch down. The fierce air turns tight and then completely still. I look up, searching for signs of where it's forming, and my breath catches in my throat. It's not a storm at all. It's a massive ship hovering above the town.

My mouth dries, turning sour as I stand frozen, watching. Forming under its wings is some kind of inky-black goo, and it looks as if it's about to ooze down. But not straight down, more like hot oil poured over a clear dome. I turn my attention back to the busy street. Parents are dragging their kids down the sidewalk or forcing them into cars or shops.

I peer back, and something similar to gears grinding from the ship cuts through the chaos. *Shit.* My palms sweat and my heart races. *What the hell is that?* Someone bumps into my shoulder. A couple darts into the alley across the street, running between the two buildings. A loud shot pierces the air, and I look back up just in time to see something shoot out of the ship.

My heart slams against my chest so hard, as if the shot hit me dead center. And then another shot, and another. The ship is rapidly shooting like a machine gun in one of my video games. A dizziness drenches me with sweat when the ammo hits the ground in an earth-shattering quake and then rolls like a huge white ball. One of the balls stops a few feet from me. It contorts, forming into a creature. My knees nearly buckle as I watch it shake goo off itself and then take flight. It soars low, chasing anyone that moves.

Holy shit! I need to get to Amy.

I turn with a scream lodged in my throat and then stop, frozen. One of those creatures is five feet in front of me. It looks just like a massive white bat. About the size of a toddler. It shrills, and a mom a few feet to my left pushes her son protectively behind her. The bat shrills again and turns to the lady. It dives headfirst into her, knocking her to the ground. Within seconds, two more bats land, fighting with the first one to feed off her. The boy, maybe four, locks eyes with me as if asking for my help. I want to tell him that there's nothing I can do to save her, but I don't. I don't know if it is because I can't form the words or if it is fight or flight. But I turn away and run, never looking back. Even when I hear the boy's scream.

I push through the mob of people, running straight

home. A block down, I swing myself around the street sign and collide with a kid on a skateboard, slamming my head on a fire hydrant. The street sign above me blurs, and my stomach churns with nausea as I try to get up. But something hits me hard in the back, forcing me back down. *Did someone just step on me?*

I stretch my arm out, searching for the hydrant to help myself up, and a blur races by me. And then another and another, and just as I try to pull myself up, something cracks against my skull.

CHAPTER SEVEN

3:10 P.M.

NORA

As I enter the theater, my stomach churns at the scent of stale popcorn and nachos from yesterday's showing. I swallow the acid burn down and wave at Gina, who is sitting on a stool behind the concession, reading a book. She barely acknowledges me. I guess it's a good thing the theater is closed today.

I go right, taking the narrow staircase slowly. The air thickens with dust. I stop halfway up and hold my middle as the pain in my stomach sharpens at the thought of losing my job. I can't even imagine what I'll do if it comes to that. I swallow the thought and continue up.

At the top, I shake my hands out, glancing between the two doors. The one on the right is the owner's office and the one to my left is the projection room. I turn left, and inside a cramped room is Mr. Gibson, hunched over a machine. I hesitate in the doorway, fidgeting with my overall straps, trying to control my breathing, but it's hard. Mr. Gibson is already the type that has a lot of opinions.

I've been caught in one of his rants more times than I can count. Mostly about the government. Then you add on that he's a big, burly guy with a long, bushy beard. He's friggin' intimidating.

With one last slow sip of air, I manage to step fully inside. I walk over to the stool near the small, window-like hole the projector is aimed at, sit, and say, "Hey."

Mr. Gibson lifts his blond head and eyes me like I'm in trouble. My stomach drops, and I cup my hands under my armpits. *Crap. Did he already speak to Mr. Stabby?*

He wipes his grease-covered hands on a red rag and then snaps it playfully at my feet. "Didn't I tell you to stop wearing those flip-flops to work?"

My shoulders burn with relief. *Thank goodness he isn't mad. At least about Mr. Stabby. Now I have a chance.*

"At least you're finally wearing the overalls I gave you." He raises a bushy blond eyebrow at me with half amusement and half disappointment. "Even though you cut them at the knees."

"Yeah, but these are more comfortable and a lot cooler than those work boots you bought me. And the overalls were way too heavy. I had to cut them."

He scowls, combing fat fingers through his beard with his voice low and growly. "Yeah, and when you slice off one of those toes, mowing or hauling shit, you're going to wish you'd worn those boots. Or when a rock from mowing or weed eating hits those bare legs, you'll regret it."

Mr. Gibson goes back to fiddling with the machine, and the movie reel sort of spins and then catches, grinding to a stop. "Come on." Mr. Gibson reaches for a smaller wrench, twisting nuts and bolts and whatever else a projector has. Then he straightens, facing me. "Wait. Why are you here? Shouldn't you still be at Flynt's place?"

"Yeah, about that," I reply, hooking my thumbs around the straps of my overalls. "There was an incident. So, I came straight here."

"Damnit, Nora. Flynt is one of my best clients." He tosses the wrench into the toolbox and glares at me. "What did you do now?"

Heat rushes to my cheeks as I straighten on the stool, ready to defend myself. "Why are you assuming it was me?" I nearly squeal, my voice cracking.

He angles his head, shooting me with an *I know how you are* look, and I get it. I've fouled up plenty of jobs. I'm lucky I still have one. Well, for now. I might not have one after I tell him what happened.

"Okay, fair. But this time it wasn't me." I fling my hand at the door. "That freak—" A loud crash sounds downstairs, like someone is smashing the concession stand up with a baseball bat. A scream rips up the staircase, followed by a loud, squeaky chirp like a mouse. "Sounds like Gina found a mouse."

"Sounds like it. Stay here." He steps out the door, but before he heads down the stairs, he spins on his heel, slamming the door shut with a curse as he leans against it with wild eyes. "Hurry and get me my phone, will ya?" His voice trembles as he points at the machine.

My mouth tugs into a small grin. Mr. Gibson is the toughest dude I've ever met. I can't believe he's afraid of a mouse, or maybe it's a rat. I slide off the stool, my grin widening. "You don't have to call an exterminator. I can go down and take care of it." I grab his phone, and the face glows with a message from Mr. Stabby. *Crap.*

"It's not a mouse, Nora."

"Sorry, rat." I stretch my arm out, and his phone blares and vibrates in my hand. Mr. Gibson grabs his phone, but not before I see what it says.

My mouth parts. *What if it's military? What if they are the reason for the black spot over the sun?*

Mr. Gibson thumbs at his phone, totally ignoring me, and then curses again, moving slightly away from the door. Then he thinks better of it. He aims his phone high in the air. I reach for my own phone to text Amy. She would know. Her dad is some bigwig in the military. Then I remember it's in the truck.

The overhead light flickers, and I lift my chin, watching the bulb sway and blink. "Mr. Gibson." I inch out from under it and flinch when the movie reel pops with sparks flying out of it. I face Mr. Gibson, searching for some type of explanation, but he seems more interested in his phone. He's probably reading Mr. Stabby's message. Thankfully, I got here first.

The stink of burned metal and plastic fills the room, and I turn back to the projector. It's spinning fast, with smoke billowing out of it. "Mr. Gibson."

He drags a hand down his face with another curse. "Where's the truck, Nora?"

The screaming moves into the theater area.

"In front of the pawnshop," I mutter, moving carefully

back to the stool, avoiding the overhead light. I step around the stool to peer out the small window.

Someone is running down the aisle. I squint, trying to see in the semi-dark theater. *Is that Gina?* Behind her is something big and scary looking, like Mr. Stabby's dog is chasing her. It's running at her so fast it looks like it's flying.

He found me! Fear vibrates down my back as I turn to Mr. Gibson. *I need to tell him about Mr. Stabby. Maybe he can help me.*

Mr. Gibson peers up and his hazel eyes are set in determination. He no longer looks scared, but serious. His jaw is working overtime as he practically looks right through me.

Did he tell Mr. Stabby I was here? Are they working together?

My stomach drops. It all makes sense now. Why Mr. Gibson is always so curious about me. Always asking where I'm going. When I'll be back. My home life. Basically wanting to know where I am all the time.

I wet my lips, searching over his shoulder. He's pressed against the door. There's no way I can get past him. The light flickers, swaying faster. Mr. Gibson's face is darker. Meaner. I back up, forced against the wall. My pulse races and my breathing grows heavier as the air thickens with smoke. I feel claustrophobic. Dizzy. I run my hand along the wall until my fingers brush the edge of the small window. It's a long way down, but it's my only option.

"We need to go." Mr. Gibson takes a large step forward.

I turn to the window and grip the edge, about to force

myself through when I see Gina fall. Mr. Stabby's dog leaps, landing on top of her, and a fierce chirp clicks, drawing my eyes up. Ten feet away are two large birds soaring. They chirp again, flapping in my direction. I pull my head back inside just in time. One of the birds hits the window, screeching. It's stuck. I clamp both hands over my mouth. *Holy crap! What is that?* It looks like a giant bat about the size of a child. Its body swollen and covered in thick oozing white goo, like it just clawed its way out of some friggin' egg. There are no eyes or ears. Instead, it has some strange nostrils where they should be. The creature struggles inside the small window, shrieking. My eyes grow with terror.

"Let's go!" Mr. Gibson wraps his hand around my arm, tight and demanding as he jerks me around. My heart beats so fast, I stumble trying to follow him down the narrow staircase.

Once we reach the front area, everything is wrecked. The concession stand is smashed. Popcorn and candy are everywhere. Shattered glass covers the red carpet, and as I crunch along, the world outside turns fierce. Car alarms, horns, and police sirens blare. Tires screech. Explosions blast. Screams pierce the air. My body shakes violently as I'm pulled out of the building and straight into the confusion. I'm so terrified, I don't even know how I'm friggin' walking, but I am.

A woman with two kids bumps into my shoulder, and I flinch, trying to run in the opposite direction, but I'm pulled back. No matter how hard I try to run away and join the others fleeing, I'm yanked forward.

I finally make it to the end of Main Street, a block from the theater, and I duck into the alley. I glance over my shoulder, and when I turn back, I'm forced against the side of the brick building, between two large trash bins. I fall to my knees and crawl between them, but I'm yanked back up. And that's when I see a fist tightly wrapped around the straps of my overalls. Mr. Gibson's holding me upright.

"Nora, look at me," he says, raising his voice over the noise. His hardened face is set in concern and something similar to anger. "Stop screaming."

I clamp my mouth shut, rubbing at my raw, sore throat as my eyes widen, darting around the alley.

"Nora." He yanks me closer, and I settle my gaze on him.

"I'm sorry," I say, but my tongue is dry and sticky, and my words come out weak and broken. I don't even think he heard me.

"Nora, we need to get to my house where my bunker is, but I can't hold you like this." Mr. Gibson catches his breath and faces me. "I need you to run on your own, got it?" I nod continuously, and he pulls me so close I can smell the sweat and grease on him. "Don't stop for anyone, Nora. I mean no one. Not even for—"

A dizziness drenches me with sweat when something hits the ground in an earth-shattering quake, mere feet from us. A massive white glob, similar to a ball of snot, lifts up, shaking itself like a dog does when it is wet. A creature emerges from it. Large wings flap out, splattering the two buildings with white goo, leaving the creature covered in slick, wet skin. Sharp, long claws grow out of the wings, diving into the pavement. The concrete splits as it anchors the claws in, stretching, and spiky bones ripple down its back. It lifts its snout with what appears to be a yawn, and a mix of white and black goo drips from razor-sharp teeth.

Mr. Gibson presses a shaky finger to his lips and then pushes me protectively behind him. I suck in a deep inhale through my nose with my hands bruising my cheeks in a tight hold, and slam my eyes shut, mentally willing this all to go away. Out of nowhere, my ears ring and pop, and then nothing, like the world went silent. No screaming. Muffled shouting. Hurried footsteps. Sirens. Nothing. Every sound has stopped, like a horror movie on pause.

It feels like an eternity as I stand behind Mr. Gibson, holding my breath, too scared to move or even swallow, in case someone hits the Play button. But I can no longer hold my breath, and a whimper vibrates out of me.

I open my eyes, and the movie explodes into action.

The creature lunges, barreling into Mr. Gibson, and I'm pushed backward with force. I fall onto my rear with a hard thud, and I quickly scramble back up. The sight before me literally scares the pee out of me. Mr. Gibson is on his back, one hand gripped tightly on a wing, while the other wing flaps violently. Mr. Gibson jabs a screwdriver deep into its torso. But it isn't doing any damage. It's like he's trying to force the screwdriver into a metal plate.

I blink. Something warm and wet splatters onto my face.

When I wipe it off, blood smears against my fingers. A scream shakes me to the core, and fight-or-flight kicks in. With my heart racing out of control, I quickly reach into the front pocket of my overalls and pull out my box knife. I slide the razor out and with all my force, I jab the blade at the creature, missing my target. I only managed to clip its wing. Smoke curls from the cut like I scorched the skin, and the smell coming off of it stinks of rotten eggs.

It whips its head at me. My eyes widen in horror as I inch backward. All four nostrils sniff in my direction. I'm about to stab it again, but it soars awkwardly upward, bouncing between the two brick buildings, releasing a high-frequency chirp.

CHAPTER EIGHT

3:21 P.M.

NORA

Once we are inside the truck, Mr. Gibson pulls out of the space, yanks the gear into drive, spins the wheel, and then slams his foot onto the gas pedal. He veers around a wreckage, and I reach for the handle above me, holding on for dear life as the truck bounces me around.

"I told you something bad was coming, didn't I?"

I nod, holding the box knife tightly in my other hand, numb and unable to think clearly. It seems so unreal. As if the chaos around me isn't even happening. It's just a bad dream, and I'll wake up soon. Everything is a blur, even the sounds, if that's possible. I look out the passenger-side window, wondering how many of those things dropped. From the looks of it, it had to be hundreds. Nothing less could have caused this much destruction in such a short amount of time. Every direction I look there is devastation. The streets are completely obscured with wrecked cars, people screaming, and huge holes where the creatures landed.

Movement overhead has me lifting my gaze. The sky is dark and blurry, like my eyes aren't focused all the way. I stretch and blink. Those aren't clouds.

I reach to grab hold of Mr. Gibson but only catch air. I can't even form words for what I'm seeing.

"Nora." Mr. Gibson grabs my arm, and I pull my gaze off the black ship. "Snap out of it."

I face forward and my stomach drops. "Watch out!"

He jerks the wheel, and we swerve, grinding along the curb, trying to avoid the pile of cars crammed along the next street.

I twist in the seat, looking at the dazed people in the middle of the street. Others are running frantically. "Mr. Gibson, we should stop and help them. I think some are really hurt."

"No. We have to get to the bunker." He swerves again, slamming me into the door.

"Screw that." I twist to grab hold of the door handle.

Before I can open the door, Mr. Gibson slams on the brakes, gripping me tight. He squeezes my wrist so hard, my fingers go numb. "I promised your mom I'd watch over you, and I have. And I will continue to do so. But if you get out of this truck, girl, I will hog-tie you and bring you right back. We are not going to stop and help anyone. Not yet."

My chin trembles at the mention of my mom, and I release the handle. I always knew they were close friends. I mean, Mom grew up here. She knew everyone, just like I do.

"I know it's harsh, but this is how we survive." I give another nod, rubbing the sore spot on my wrist. His tone softens. "I'm sorry, but the world we know is no longer.

Now it's kill or be killed, and not just with those creatures. Men. Women." He turns into his neighborhood with a quick glance at me. "Even kids younger than you will be after what's ours. I'm counting on you to do what's necessary when the time comes."

I hold back tears. I know what he's asking of me. I clench my jaw with bile threatening and squint at him. What a disappointment I will be when the time comes. *I won't kill for you.* I lower my gaze and catch sight of blood seeping through his shirt.

"You're hurt," I say.

"It's fine." He drives down his street so fast that when he jerks the wheel, he nearly crashes through his garage door. But it lifts just in time for Mr. Gibson to pull into the garage and jam the gear in park. "Let's go. We have a lot to do."

My hand freezes on the door handle as I stare at the corner of the garage, at the wires threading through the wood, leading down into the bunker. I knew Mr. Gibson had a bunker. It's not like he kept it a secret. He's pretty much known as the survivalist guy, but everyone, including myself, thought it was somewhere out in the woods. So, you can imagine my surprise when I stumbled across it last spring.

I was here looking for more supplies, and a bottle of algae remover rolled under the sofa. Nearly pooped my heart out when I discovered his bunker. I immediately asked him about it. Of course, I didn't ask very nicely. I think I even called it his dungeon. That's when he told me it was his bunker. He even showed me around the outside and told me about the solar panels and everything that keeps it going. But when it came to actually going down into it, I gave some excuse and hightailed it out of here.

Plus, at the time, he gave me the heebie-jeebies like something was off with him. The way he watched me or bought me stuff. I've been in plenty of bad foster homes. I know how this goes. It's why I keep a safe distance from everyone now. If you know all the risks and never put yourself in any of those situations, it makes it harder, right? Of course, Amy said I was being paranoid, yet again. And now I get it. He was doing as Mom asked. I mean, it's Mr. Gibson. I've been alone with him loads of times since then, even in his house, and nothing bad ever happened. Now that I think about it, Mr. Gibson is probably the safest person to be alone with. He keeps his distance. A lot of room to run if needed. Heck, he's never even touched me, until today. Amy's right, I am—

Amy!

I straighten, plucking my phone out of the dash mount, and hop out of the truck. "What about Amy and Chief Mori? We can't leave them." I think of Ethan and remember his dad is usually home about this time. He should be okay, but still. "And the Bains family."

Mr. Gibson jumps into the truck bed. "I know, and when it settles down, I'll go out and get them." He unlatches the silver box in the back of the truck and reaches inside it. "I'm sure Chief Mori has them both in the safe room."

"That's right. I forgot about that," I mutter, reading Amy's text.

Guilt squeezes my ribs for never telling Amy about the safe room, but Mr. Gibson had sworn me to secrecy. I couldn't tell her. It was part of my job. One I hope to have for a long while. Next year, Amy will go off to college, and I'll still be here. I need this job.

"They'll be fine for a while. But for now, I need to get you inside and tend to my wound, okay?"

"Okay."

My racing heart slows somewhat as I text her back.

NORA

> A safe room? That's crazy. This whole thing is crazy. I'm with Mr. Gibson and we are coming to get you soon. I can't wait to see you. Stay safe.

I shove the phone into my back pocket, knowing the second it quiets out here, I'm going after her and her mom. Even if her mom hates me.

Mr. Gibson hands me a small black bag, while he pulls out a bulkier one. "Close the garage door, will ya?"

"Yeah." I walk around the back end of the truck, making my way past pool chemicals and tools for the door that leads into the house. I press the garage door button, and I can't help but grieve the world we are about to lock out. But what else am I supposed to do? My chin trembles uncontrollably as I watch the door slide shut.

Mr. Gibson walks over to the dirty, old sofa, bends and digs under it, then lifts the whole thing up. Under it is a secret staircase, like a storm cellar. He walks down the dark stairs where only a trickle of light filters in. I slowly descend after him, watching him punch in the code. 6482. The hatch makes a sucking sound, and I take the last step.

"In you go."

I walk past a security area and into what I assume is the living room. Against the right side of the wall is a mustard-colored loveseat made of velvet. On both sides are dark brown end tables with lamps that match the loveseat in color and texture. Across from it sits an old-fashioned television. Maybe from the 1980s. Shooting up behind it are antennas with foil covering the ends. On the left side of the TV is a bar with liquor lined on a shelf, and under it is a record player with a crate of records beside it. To the right of the TV are loads of books on a built-in bookcase with board games and puzzles.

I walk by the sofa, straight into the kitchen, and then turn right, down one of the beehive-looking tunnels. There's a small greenhouse with blue barrels lined against the wall. I retrace my steps, walking through the kitchen and back into the living quarters.

"Your room is down that way." He points to his left at another beehive-looking tunnel.

How big is this place?

Wait. Did he say, my room?

I start down the hallway and then stop halfway through. My heart drops. The door on my left has a small wooden sign hanging on it. *Nora.* I quickly back away, chewing on my thumbnail. I spit a sliver of nail onto the floor, staring at the door. Maybe I shouldn't have trusted him. I glance over my shoulder. Mr. Gibson is sitting at the kitchen table, prying open a large container.

What would Amy do?

She would tell me to stop being paranoid and go help him.

He pulls out a medical book, flipping through it. *I don't know if I can trust him. I mean, what sane person builds a bunker, adding a room for a teenage girl?*

Killers! That's who.

I go back to evening out my thumbnail and taste blood. *Crap!* I fold my thumb into my overalls, trying to stop the bleeding as I debate my options.

Should I risk my life by staying down here or take my chances with the monsters?

Either way, up or down, I'm probably a goner.

"Nora. In the living quarters, there's a bottle of vodka at the bar. Fetch it for me, will ya?"

"Yeah, sure," I squeak, blinking the worst-case scenario away, and walk into the living room. When I move over to Mr. Gibson, his face is dull, almost lifeless. He's not doing well. I know this is really bad to think about, but if he's this bad off, at least he can't friggin' hurt me.

"Here," I say, handing him the bottle.

He takes the bottle, twisting the lid off, and then dips his head back, taking a long swig of it.

I pull out the other chair, and Mr. Gibson grabs my arm. "Hey, I ain't in no shape to do what needs to be done. I need you to go over to the security nook and grab the black book. It has everything you need to know about this place. It will tell you in detail everything that needs to be done."

"What? No way. I'll mess it all up."

He squeezes my arm gently. "It has Chief Mori's information in there. You'll be able to contact them."

My heart leaps into my throat. Maybe I can trust him. Maybe he's the first adult in my life that I can trust.

"Okay." I start forward, and a loud curse rips out of him as he pours the liquid onto his wound. I turn back, dropping into the chair, watching him take too many swigs of vodka, and then trying to thread a needle. My heart goes out to him. Stupid empathy.

"Here, let me help." I scoot the chair closer and reach for the needle and thread.

"Thank you, Nora. You're a good girl. You don't deserve the shit you've been through." He takes another swig. "I know you've had it hard with your mom, and I . . . " He glances down the hall, following my line of sight, then he looks back at me. "The room . . . I only added it because you're the only family I have." His head dips, and his breathing is shallow. "I loved your mom, but she never loved me back. I don't think she's ever loved anyone but you."

"Ha!" I disagree, and he holds up a hand.

"I'm serious. When she found out she was pregnant, she came straight home. To me. And she stayed off that shit for a long time. But it's a disease, Nora. One that has always had a hold on your mom."

"Yeah, well, it must be strangling her right now." I pull the thread through the small hole, tying the ends off.

"I'm sure it is, but you understand she can't help it, right?"

The only thing I understand is: When you've been thrown away as many times as I have, you learn there isn't anyone you can count on, but yourself. And to protect myself from harm, I can't allow anyone to place me back into the system. Heck, I've been in the system more times than I've been with her. And the government's so-called system is crap. It's either church-going foster dads who like to bully kids around or lock them in rooms for days. Or you work your tail end off until you drop, hoping you've earned enough time for a sandwich.

And don't get me started on the foster parents that are good. Those are so few that when I did land in one, I wasn't there very long. A week tops. Then the judge would yank me out and place me back with Mom because she sobered up, said how she was better now. And she was for the first week or so, and then the cycle began all over again. It was a beer here and a needle there. Within months, she'd decide I wasn't worth it and would move without me, yet again. The system sucks and has failed me too many times to trust anyone again. I won't go back. Ever.

But I don't say any of this. He doesn't know how bad it's been for me. No one does, but Amy. And that's why the second I can I'm out the door, going after her. With or without Mr. Gibson.

Instead, I nod and reach for the small scissors.

"Hey." I look up, and his eyes are red and wet. "You don't ever have to go back. Your secret is safe with me."

My throat catches. *Does he know?*

"Why do you think you always came back? Here, to this town and to your mom. Because I made her. I even offered to take you in once, but she refused. Said she had it handled."

"Clearly, she didn't." I try to laugh it off, but my words come out in a croak.

"Well, now you have a safe place." He takes another long swig. "You never have to worry about any of that ever again. Not as long as I'm alive." He puts the bottle down and sits taller in the chair. "Now, come on." He slaps his chest, right under his collarbone. "Let's get this taken care of and then go fetch the Mori family and a few others. I don't know about you, but I'd like some more people down here."

My chin trembles with a mix of emotions. I feel awful for what I thought about him, but also touched that he thinks of me as family. *Why didn't he ever just friggin' say so?* I look down to the clothes he's bought me and think back to the basic essentials, like toothpaste or deodorant, he's given me, saying he bought the wrong brand. I guess in a way he did. I was just too stubborn and paranoid to see it. Instead, I thought he was grooming me or something. I brush the tears away and push to my feet, my hands shaky but ready.

Now, it's my turn to take care of him.

CHAPTER NINE
3:21 P.M.

AMY

Shit! No electricity. Luckily, there's enough light coming from the windows to see as I move into the hallway. There's so much noise happening outside, fear shoots through me. Car alarms. Dogs barking. People screaming.

Mom's going to be pissed that I left the safe room.

I walk into the living room, and an orange tint peeks through the window like it's late evening, not three in the afternoon. Leaning against the back of the sofa, I peer through the curtain. My breath catches. Across the street, a car has rammed into a fire hydrant, and water shoots into the air. Looking farther down the street, Tommy from school races by, screaming, as some large bird flies after him. The bird catches Tommy, pecking at his neck, while he flails, trying to escape. Then the bird lifts him high in the air. I cup my mouth, frozen in terror. *What the hell is that?*

"Chief Mori!" I flinch at the loud banging on the front door. "Amy!"

It's my neighbor, Mrs. Blanchard. I push off the sofa and hurry my steps, but when I reach for the doorknob, Mom's voice hijacks my movements. *"If someone is banging on the door for help and you're home alone, do not open the door. It could be a trap, or whoever is after them could break in here and hurt you both. Call the police, but don't open the door. Ever."* I've heard these words my entire life growing up, but I've never listened to them. I cut my eyes to the window, in the direction Tommy was attacked. My hand slides off the doorknob as I steal a step backward.

"Please let me in. One of those things is out here," she says in desperation, banging harder on the door.

One of those birds? How many are out there?

I inch away. Something hits the other side of the door so hard, Mrs. Blanchard screams. I jump, bumping into the hall table. The vase of flowers crashes onto the floor.

Mom, where are you?

I quickly reach down, grabbing one of the large shards and take a silent step backward.

Mom, why did you leave me like this?

With a tight grip on the shard, I drop to my knees, holding the weapon straight out in front of me.

Do you even care?

Tears slide down my cheeks as I rock back and forth on my heels, praying Mom comes back soon.

Is your job so much more important than me?

Are you even coming back?

My chin trembles uncontrollably, and a breathless squeak hurts my throat.

I scan the living room to my right, the front door, and then the dining room to my left. A cold sweat drenches me.

Please come back.

I face the front door, and my breathing skips every few seconds, just like my heart. I'm scared. Every sound invades my senses. The muffled screaming outside. The sharp, continuous shrill of the siren. The grandfather clock, ticking loudly in the dining hall. They mingle and throb in my ears. I want to block it out, but I'm too scared to move. My skin crawls and my vision blurs as the minutes tick by.

I can't stay here. I need to go back to the safe room.

When I shakily lift up, a crash against the door causes it to burst open. A scream rips out of me as Mrs. Blanchard falls onto what's left of the door.

I shuffle against the hallway table. My heart's erratic. I fear it might explode. I grip the shard tight, and my palm stings as I wait for whatever attacked her to come for me. I hold my breath, straining my ears. It doesn't sound like anything is in the house but Mrs. Blanchard. All the chaos is outside.

I brave a peek around the table. She isn't moving.

Is she dead?

I silently put down the shard to creep onto my hands, about to crawl over to her, and she scratches at the linoleum. I immediately stop, balancing on my hands and knees.

"Mrs. Blanchard?" I stutter out.

She gurgles something like *done* or *gun.*

Is she choking? Should I help her?

I don't know what to do.

A gut-wrenching scream pierces the air. My eyes shoot up. Outside, Mrs. Miller runs across my lawn, carrying her youngest and practically dragging her oldest. Seconds later, Mr. Miller races by, covered in blood.

What is happening?

Mrs. Blanchard moves, drawing my eyes back to her. She lifts a bare shoulder in a twitching fit, and something crawls under her skin.

Holy shit! I slowly lean back on my heels, rubbing my hands along my thighs, watching.

Please hurry, Momma.

Mrs. Blanchard lurches into a crouching position, sniffing the air. When she turns her head, half of her neck is torn out. Another scream slips out of me, and her dazed, bloodshot eyes anchor onto me, wide and alert.

I cup my mouth, breathing heavily. Her mouth opens so wide it looks like she's trying to eat her own face. I cry out in fear, and we both bolt upright.

She is no longer the prey.

I am.

I turn, sprinting down the hallway and straight into Mom's office, knocking everything off the desk, hoping to slow her down. I slide on paperwork and folders, staggering and trying to catch myself just as an explosion cuts the air. My heart drops with fear prickling my skin.

"Are you okay?"

The sound of Mom's voice forces my quivering chin down. I turn around, and Mom is standing in the doorway with a shotgun aimed out in front of her.

She steps over Mrs. Blanchard, striding quickly toward me. "Did she bite you?"

I shake my head, frozen in place, staring at Mrs. Blanchard's dead body.

"Come on," Mom says, pulling on my arm. She guides me back into the safe room. "I thought I told you not to leave the safe room or open the door." She removes her police belt and slings it onto the security desk. Then punches a code in a safe, opening it.

"I need to get to the county sheriff and tell him what's going on." After she places her glock and ankle gun into the safe, she peers up at me.

"Are you listening to me?"

I don't say anything or even nod that I understand, because I don't. I just stand next to her, shaking as she reloads the shotgun. She pulls down a brown backpack, rummages through it, and then grabs a shit ton of ammo, shoving that into the bag. It isn't until she yanks off her black police shirt that I snap out of it. Beneath it, her white T-shirt is stained red.

"Oh my God. Are you hurt?" I ask, moving closer.

"No, it's not mine."

I step away from the shirt lying on the floor. *What does that even mean?*

Whose blood is it?

"Put this on," she tells me, shoving the bag into my chest.

"Mom, what is going on? What are those things?" I reach for my laptop and phone, sliding them into the pack.

"We'll talk about that once we're somewhere safe. But for now, I need you to stay calm." She cups my face with fear etched across hers. "I mean it. Okay, baby?"

Tears roll down her cheeks, and my chest squeezes. Every emotion hits me at once, but none rise to the surface. I don't know what to feel first.

"Just tell me what's going on. Please. What are those things? Whose blood is that? Did you hurt someone?"

She looks at me for a moment. Her eyes pool with more tears, and my own threaten.

"Mom, talk to me."

"I will the second we're out of here, but for now, I need you to stay right behind me." She grabs my arm, strong but not painfully. Her hands are ice cold. "Whatever happens or whatever you see, do not run away from me. Got it?" Mom isn't just scared, she's petrified.

"Mom, why can't we just stay in here? The generator is back on. We can just ride it out here until help arrives."

"Help isn't coming, Amy. And if we don't leave now, we'll be trapped. There's a shield coming down over our town, and we have to get out and warn everyone. And we have to go on foot. My car is trashed. Most are."

"What do you mean? I don't understand. Mom, please—"

"Amy!" Mom says in a harsh whisper. "For once, just stop talking and do what I say. *Please*." Her voice hitches on the last word as she squeezes my arm.

I give a firm nod, and Mom guides me toward the doorway. She peeks around the doorframe and then leads me out of the house.

It's nearly dark outside now. *How is that possible?* I start to reach for the flashlight on my phone, but the sound of wings flapping grabs my attention. Above us, a bunch of large birds are circling our town.

Mom yanks me forward, guiding me down the road. My eyes widen as one of those birds dive-bombs someone in the distance, and then another one, and another. *Holy shit!* I try to flee, but Mom tightens her grip, pulling me along as we walk quietly across the street. We sneak behind Mr. Reid's home, toward the back alley, and straight into the woods.

Once we're inside, shielded by even more darkness, Mom turns to me. A cold chill swirls around us.

"Now, we run and don't stop, got it?" She grips my shoulders tightly. "I mean it, Amy. If I go down, do not stop. Keep going."

She doesn't wait for me to reply or even nod. She grips my arm now and takes off running. We weave around dead logs, jump over fallen branches. All while wings flap violently above us. I look skyward, at the large bird circling the treetops.

I trip, skidding across pine needles, twigs, and rocks, scraping my knees and hands. Mom turns back for me, but so does the bird. It's diving straight down. Panic shoots through me. Mom's raw and desperate voice screams for me to run.

I quickly push to my feet.

"Hurry!" Mom shouts, shooting at the bird.

I look over my shoulder and up. Its wings viciously beat, trying to gain speed as it zeroes in on me. Mom's bullets ricochet off it. My heart skips, then pounds painfully as I force myself to run faster. It's gaining closer. Fear burns in my chest. Everything blurs.

All I can think is, *run, run, run*.

Behind me, Mom fires again, and it lets out a chirp so loud my teeth vibrate. I don't look back. I push myself harder than I ever have, lengthening my strides, jumping over branches, and weaving in and out of trees. And with each step, I lose more light.

When I make it to Dover's Bridge, dividing Canyon Falls and Ark City, I slow my pace at the ink-black substance slowly oozing down in front of me like a shield.

Ten feet from it, I finally turn. "Mom?" My voice is so

raw, it doesn't even sound like me. I spin in a tight circle. It's nearly pitch black now.

Where is she?

"Don't stop. That's our way out."

I turn to her voice. I can barely make out Mom's silhouette.

"Mom?"

At full speed, Mom grabs my arm, never stopping, and I'm yanked forward. As we duck beneath the oozing shield, my heart beats so hard it hurts. Everything hurts.

I bend, bracing myself on my knees, and see black boots stop on the other side.

Who is that?

Before I can think more on it, the goo hits the ground in an earth-shattering quake. Dirt coughs up around me as the ground splits, racing toward me like roots stretching and strengthening. Desperate, I scramble backward before the crack reaches me. Then it stops.

I sway, dizzy and near faint, as the shield hardens, cracking like water freezing, sealing everyone in on the other side.

"Stop!"

I turn to my mom's voice. She's jumping up and down, waving a car to stop. I look back to the shield. Whoever it was, I really hope that bird thing doesn't get them. A police vehicle with *County Sheriff* painted on the side slows to a stop. Mom walks toward the driver's side to speak to the officer as I move off the road, hugging myself.

"Chief Mori," Mom says, shaking the man's hand. "I don't know much, other than they look like bats. Massive ones. About half the size of me." She wipes her mouth. "And, there's a lot of them. They're killing anyone that runs." Mom's voice shakes as she talks really fast. "I don't believe they can see or hear, but they are definitely picking something out about us in order to find us. And from what I could see, nothing kills them, not even guns. The only ones you can kill are the people who have been bitten and have turned. One of my deputies was bitten, and he tried to attack me."

"Turned?"

Mom bends, bracing herself on her knees, gulping in air, and then replies, "If you're bitten, you change into something similar to . . . I don't know, a zombie. Whatever it is, they chase and attack you just like the bats." Mom wets her lips with a hiccup and straightens. "Did it hit everywhere, or just here?"

A wave of guilt and adoration swims in my belly as I watch Mom. I should have known she would come for me. That she was protecting me by putting me in the safe room. It's my own stupid fault I left. I can't be mad at that. At her. Especially after how much she learned about these things in such a short amount of time. She must be really good at her job. I guess that's why everyone trusts her so much. But damn, why can't she give me some of that attention and shit?

The county sheriff doesn't answer Mom's question. Instead, he gets out of the police car. As they move off onto the other side of the road, I glance over at the black shield. With my heart in my throat, the tears finally spill out.

Nora!

CHAPTER TEN

5:08 P.M.

AMY

Mom ushered me into the back of the sheriff's car over an hour ago. I hate it. This is the second time she has locked me in something. If I could, I'd get out again, but apparently Mom wants me to stay safe. Or she doesn't trust me to stay. Which, I guess, she has reason to.

I chew on a thick chunk of my hair, hugging the backpack close to my chest, watching the police and Mom. All of whom are standing on one side of the yellow tape, shouting at a crowd on the other side. Most of them are people from our town, parents that work in Ark City and a few reporters. They're demanding answers or shouting theories. So far, I've heard several, from an alien invasion to war with another country, even a scientific experiment gone wrong. All remind me of Nora. She's probably freaking out right now.

God, I hope she's still alive.

I shove the backpack onto the floorboard, then grip my

phone tightly in my lap. I can't stop my hands from shaking. Hell, every part of me is cold and trembling.

A loud rumbling sounds from behind the squad car, and I turn in the seat, looking out the back window. The crowd splits, moving off to the side of the road, muttering to each other.

Holy shit! It's the military.

My heart skips at the black SUV. *Is it Dad? I really hope Shin is with him!* I lean against the seat for a better look.

A dude with a bunch of stuff pinned to his uniform hops out of the truck. *Nope, not Dad.* I slump against the seat, balancing my chin on my arms. *Which I'm fine with, but I really want to see my brother. I miss him so much.* I've already tried calling him and have sent him and Nora about a hundred messages. Neither have replied to me.

The military guy marches straight up to the county sheriff and Mom while soldiers start clearing people away from the area. I keep my eye on the one in charge. He says something to Mom and the county sheriff, and whatever it was, they aren't happy about it.

They march back toward me, and I grimace at the power shift. From the looks of it, neither of them is used to being told what to do. Mom's face is tight with anger, and the county sheriff repositions his cowboy hat roughly on his head.

Mom opens the door, gesturing for me to scoot over, and I ask, "What's going on?"

"Hell, if I know." Mom closes the door harder than needed, watching the military guy shout out orders. The county sheriff slides into the driver's seat. He takes off his hat, tossing it on the dash as he starts the car.

"The sheriff is going to take us to the nearest hotel." Mom faces me. "Are you okay?"

"Yes," I reply, grabbing my backpack and hugging it tight. "Are you?"

Mom pulls me close, kissing the top of my head. "I am now. But I'll feel even better once I call your dad and speak to him and Shin." She pulls her phone out, scrolls, then taps Shin's name.

Maybe she will have better luck and he will call her back.

The county sheriff reverses the police car and then speeds forward, kicking up dirt as he pulls away.

I pull a chunk of my hair close to my mouth, then drop it, knowing how much Mom hates it. Instead, I dip my chin, biting the loop of my backpack. I really hope Shin comes back with Dad. I need him more than ever now. And what about Nora?

Is she safe?

Dead?

My stomach twists with concern and fear. I'm going to throw up. I can't stop my brain from conjuring up every horrible thing that could happen.

I feel like Nora. How does she live like this? Her brain is in constant fear.

Twenty minutes later, the sheriff pulls up to an old, run-down motel, and I shudder at the state of it.

Please don't tell me we are staying here?

The front office is lined with windows, and there's so much filth caked on them, you can't even see inside. I can barely see the *Open* sign. The sheriff gets out, and I lean forward, looking past Mom. The rest of the place is just as bad, scary even. There's a row of doors leading into what looks like nine rooms, and along the cracked sidewalk, grass has sprouted. Hanging from the covered walk are a bunch of fly traps, littered with dead flies, with more circling. And there's trash everywhere. Against the building. In the parking lot. In the pool. There's even a car filled to the brim with it.

Three doors down, standing in the doorway is a toddler, wearing only a saggy diaper, sucking on a bottle. Farther down, near the last door, is a portly man bent over, working on a rusty old truck. And he doesn't seem bothered about what has happened in Canyon Falls. Maybe he doesn't know. Or maybe he's trying to fix his truck so he can leave this place. I know I would. Even if my hometown hadn't just been attacked. This place is awful.

The sheriff opens the door for us, and the second I'm out, I'm hugging my bag, scanning the area for more life. From the soda machine that says *Shasta* across the front, the strong stench of sewer in the air, the abandoned gas station across the street, to the kid staring at me, not moving from that spot. Not to mention the complete isolation here. There isn't even a business or residence around for blocks. All that's missing is a tumbleweed rolling down the dirt road. Nora would freak!

This place reminds me of the beginning of a B-rated horror flick, and we're the IT girls. We should run, and fast.

I wet my lips, agreeing with Nora's imaginary voice as I step backward, bumping into the police car. The greasy man working on the truck straightens, and I hug my backpack tighter, wishing I had listened to Mom. I should have put something else on. He reaches for a can of beer balanced on the lip of the hood and rubs his belly as he shoots me a toothless grin. I quickly turn, following Mom into the office.

It's just as bad in here as it is outside. Every fiber of my being screams to run. To get somewhere safe, and then I think of home and what has transpired. At least it's safer here than at home. I just hope Nora stays safe, too.

I swallow the uncertainty as the owner hands Mom a set of keys.

"Welp, it looks like you two are all set here," the sheriff says, sliding a stained, beige cowboy hat onto his dark curls. He reaches for the door, holding it open for us.

"Thank you, Sheriff." Mom walks out the door, and I follow.

We stop in front of the sheriff's car, Mom waiting to say bye to him and me not wanting to know which room is ours. I look to my left, at the greasy guy, and he's watching us. *Please don't be anywhere near him.*

Mom turns to me, handing me the key. "Go ahead, Amy. I'll be right along. We're in number five."

My eyes widen. *By myself!*

"Go on," she urges.

I thumb the worn leather keyring as I start forward and hear a thumping sound coming out of the toddler's room. I pass by and there's a couple, maybe in their twenties, buck naked, having sex on a table. *Jesus Christ! Close the door.*

I hurry my steps until I'm standing in front of room five. From the corner of my eye, I see the greasy guy move. *Holy shit! Is he coming this way?* My heart drops along with the key.

"Need help with that?" he asks, standing to my right.

"No," I mutter, bending for the key. When I straighten, he walks behind me to the door on my left. I push the key in, watching him walk into room four. *That's just great!* I open the door, and I'm instantly hit with the disgusting odor of stale smoke and onions. *Gross!*

I pinch my nose, staring at the two small beds with a square end table wedged between them. I move farther inside, and to my left is a dresser with a television on top of it. Straight ahead is a door. I'm guessing that's the bathroom. No way I am looking in there.

I start to toss my bag onto the olive-green bedspread, then think better of it. Instead, I lower it onto the small table near the window to my right, and my backpack dings. I quickly unzip it, fishing for my phone. I thumb through it, searching for a message, but there isn't one.

Hmm, where did it come from? Then I see my laptop. *Nora!*

I quickly peek through the curtain. Mom is still talking to the sheriff. I pull out the laptop and sit in one of the two chairs, chancing another look out the curtain before focusing on the words.

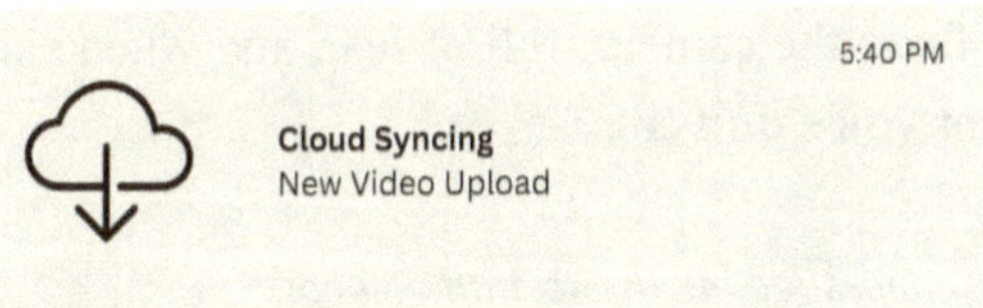

The second I see Nora, my chin quivers as tears roll down my cheeks.

Hey Ams, I know without service you probably won't get this, but I'm hoping it will come back on soon and that you have your phone. I've tried the walkie-talkie and channel Mr. Gibson gave me, but no one is answering.

I'm not sure if it works through a safe room or not, so I'm making this video in hopes it finds you.

She brushes tears off her cheeks, and I do the same.

I know what a worrywart you are when it comes to me, but I'm safe.

I lean closer to the screen, trying to see where she is, but it's really dark.

I'm with Mr. Gibson in his—

A loud chirp echoes, and I quickly turn the volume down, watching as the camera pans down at Nora's feet. The camera shakes violently, and I hear a loud chirping and banging.

I cup my mouth, stifling my breath. Seconds feel like an eternity, and then everything stops. Finally, Nora lifts the phone. I inhale deeply.

She faces the camera, full of fear, and when she speaks again, her voice quivers.

Please message me the second you can.

The video ends, and I shut the laptop, peeking through the curtain at Mom.

If I give this to her, she'll take it from me. I won't know if Nora sends another message.

I chew on my hair, staring at the laptop.

But if I don't give it to her and she finds out, I'll be in so much trouble.

My teeth grind along strands of hair.

But if I do give it to her, I won't know if Nora stays alive. Mom would never tell me.

The door opens, and Mom strides in as Police Mom. Unapproachable. Her stern face set in an expression that says *I'm not in the mood, Amy.*

"Don't chew on your hair, Amy. Find a healthier outlet."

So much for the soft and caring mom.

My shoulders tighten. I drop my hair and gaze at the laptop. "Sorry, Mom," I say through controlled anger.

I shove the laptop into my bag. Maybe if she was a little more welcoming and understanding, I might tell her about it. But she's just so . . . Mom. This must be how Shin felt before Mom shipped him off to Dad's. I even understand what he said to me before he left. *All she sees in me, Amy, are my faults.*

Mom sits on the edge of the bed, turning on the TV. I pull my legs up and hug my knees, watching her back.

Shin is right. She doesn't see who we are. What we can do. She sees only what we do wrong. I hate it.

I rest my cheek on my knee. *I hate her!* If it weren't for Nora, I'd have willingly gone with Shin. But I couldn't be another person who abandoned her. So I stayed.

CHAPTER ELEVEN

5:08 P.M.

SHIN

Oh my God, who is screaming? I lift my head, rolling onto my side, and my belly churns. In front of me, emergency lights are flashing on and off in a haze of smoke.

Oh my god, was I hit by a car?

I touch the back of my head. *Am I bleeding?* I quickly pull out my phone, and the screen glows in the darkness. *Shit! I am.*

I push to my feet and stagger, making my way toward the lights. Two cars have slammed into each other, and they're both smoking. I turn, aiming the phone light out in front of me. Someone pops out of the darkness, bumping into my shoulder, forcing me against the wreckage.

I push off the car, and my belly churns again. I'm going to be sick. I brace myself on my knees, and my body curves in a violent puke. With each heave, my head throbs. I wipe at my mouth and then straighten.

Why is it so dark outside? How long was I out?

I glance at my phone, 5 p.m. I peer up. The streetlights

aren't on. I pivot, panning the light at the sounds behind me, and then back in front of me. Standing in the middle of the road, I try to remember what happened before I was hit.

It takes a full minute to fully register as another person runs by. I aim my phone in their direction, but it's still hard to see more than a few feet. Turning back, there's a guy standing right in front of me, not moving. It's almost as if he was running with the other person and something stopped him, freezing him in place.

I start forward, and he shakes his head slightly, like he is completely terrified. I stop.

A scream rips through the air in a frightening degree, and I shakily pan the phone in that direction. There's a white mass on top of someone on the ground mere feet from me. It moves, and its snout is deep in someone's neck. My mouth opens wide, but the guy lunges, clamping a tight hand over my mouth before I can scream.

Holy shit! What kind of nightmare monster is that?

Skin so pale and translucent, I can see every black vein pulse along its long, thin torso. Its eyes are small slits with some kind of nostril right under them that flares open and closed like it's breathing. On its back are massive, ghost-like wings. It lifts its head, snorts, and blood spurts out of another set of nostrils on top of its snout. It dives back into the man's neck and, within seconds, its hollow cheeks bloom with a hint of color and fullness. Pulling in another gulp of air, its skin stretches with soft tissue growing under the forehead and cheeks, forcing muscles to develop on its face. The eye slits peel open, stretching and forming into an eyeball. The snout slides down a little, twisting and crunching, as if it's breaking the cartilage into a smaller nose, as if it is transforming into a full human right before my eyes.

My face trembles as my heart pounds, nearly exploding. I need to find Mom and Amy. I look at the guy who is clamping my mouth so hard that bruises are forming.

Someone darts past us, and the creature lifts its head, releasing a high-pitched echo that vibrates the air. It lifts off the man, standing above him, then takes off running, gaining speed, before taking flight.

Holy shit!

Within seconds, another scream penetrates the air.

I force my eyes back onto the guy in front of me. He looks calm and calculated as he scans the area. *How is he not shitting himself?*

"Follow me," he mouths, lowering his hand. At least, I think that's what he said. Even if he didn't, I am. This guy looks like he knows what to do and where he's going. I can use him to find my family.

We zigzag through town, only stopping when one of those things screams or looks our way. I feel like we're playing a really messed up game of *Red Light, Green Light*. All the while, I scan the light in front of me.

It's complete chaos. There's so many people running or lying dead on the street that I'm surprised I'm still alive. How *did* I survive this? Those things must have thought I was dead.

I aim the light at every lifeless face I pass, and my gut tightens at all the people I know. Secretly, I pray Mom or Amy aren't among them. I think of Nora, Ethan, and Asher. My throat clenches. I really hope I don't find them either.

As we walk through my old neighborhood, I'm thankful some homes still have electricity. It isn't as dark or terrifying. But I know it won't last long. The lights, or the silence out this way. Those solar panels only work if there is sunlight. I pan the light up. And apparently there isn't any sun. I only hope those creatures stay near the town square.

We finally stop at a white house, and I hesitate. This is my old house. The guy turns to me with his finger pressed against his lips.

Who is this guy? How long has he been living here?

I give a slight nod, and he turns to the door, quietly opening it. I step over the threshold, and it doesn't look like my old house. The carpet in the living room and hallway was pulled up and replaced with hardwood flooring. The dining room and kitchen aren't divided; it's one big room now.

He puts his phone into his mouth while he moves through the house, fast and efficiently, only picking up certain items and then shoving them into a bag. It's too dark to see exactly what he's packing, but some of it is food and water, and I really hope he shares. My mouth is bone dry with remnants of bile coating my tongue.

He shoulders the bag and then slides a bulky contraption over his head. *Are those night-vision goggles?* He gestures for me to follow again. And if I weren't so scared to speak, I'd tell him he doesn't need to keep telling me to follow him. I'm sticking to him like glue until I find my mom.

We move into another room, and he clears debris from the house off a tall safe. Then he opens it and pulls out a bunch of gear.

Seriously, who the hell is this guy? Military? Hope swells in my chest.

He straps on a vest and then pulls out all kinds of guns, strapping those on his hips and ankles, wherever he can find space. But the one I'm really happy to see is the rifle he slings across his chest. After he checks and double checks all the ammo, he shoves a large bag into my chest. He turns, facing me, and unzips it, pulling out a glow stick. He cracks it open, dropping it inside the bag.

"I need you to carry this bag and hand me one of these when I do this"—he lifts a hand and swirls his index finger in the air—"got it?"

I nod. He grabs the front of my jacket, pulling me along. He guides me to the back of the house, straight outside. We walk around the pool, moving to the back fence, and he opens a gate.

We walk maybe five minutes, deep into the woods, and I finally ask, "Where are we going?"

"To find my family."

I'd ask who his family is, but noticing how this guy moves and acts, I can already tell if he wanted me to know, he'd have elaborated.

He stops walking and bends, looking at the ground like he's tracking something or someone, and then something similar to tinnitus is so loud and piercing it buckles us both. I cup my ears, trying to block it out, but it's so sharp it cuts through.

The moment it stops, my ears are still ringing, and my head hurts even worse. The guy steps forward, yanking me up to my feet, and I feel nauseous all over again.

We continue on, him tracking something in the woods and me hugging this bag as if it's a shield. Every so often, he dips down, brushing leaves and twigs, and then stands up, moving again. All the while, I scan the area with my phone, keeping watch. *What the hell is he doing?* I thought he was looking for his family.

After what feels like twenty minutes, we come out of the woods and stop by a barbed wire fence.

Where are we? I'm completely turned around.

He lifts part of it up, motioning for me to go. I duck down, stepping over the lower part, then straighten, doing the same for him.

When I turn around, the beam of light cuts through the dark, and I catch sight of a trailer. I know where we are now. This guy maneuvers through a line of uneven rows of trailers. I follow, walking backward, keeping the light always moving. Even though it seems as if we are the only ones in this area, I hate being here. There's too many shadows and corners for one of those things to hide in. Not to mention walking on this gravel is loud as shit.

I turn around, and this guy has stopped right in front of Nora's place. My gut knots. I thought he was looking for his family. He aims his rifle as he walks up the saggy porch.

Fear vibrates down my back, and not from the creaky wood under my boot. How does he know the Browns? Is he one of Nora's mom's boyfriends?

He tests the doorknob, and when it doesn't twist open, he mutters a curse. Sidestepping, he peers into the window as I scan the porch. The potted plants and flowers that usually hang off the beams are gone. Along with the lawn chairs and the pile of shoes that are usually shoved under them. I glance down. The *Piss Off* mat is gone too. Is this still Nora's place? Maybe Nora and her mom moved, and his family lives here now.

The guy mutters another curse and steps back. He pauses, looking back and forth, then he lifts a boot, kicking the door in. I nearly shit my heart out at the loud noise. *What the fuck is wrong with him?*

I instantly turn, scanning the area with heavy pants. When I turn back, the guy is already inside, searching the place. I join him, and it feels abandoned. The usual heavy scent of flowery perfume from Nora's mom is gone. Now, dust tickles my nose. The place is a disaster, like someone left in a hurry. Pieces of furniture in the living room are missing and what's left is overturned or broken.

I walk into the kitchen, and the table is broken, leaning against the wood panel. I pan the light up, and the shelves are empty. No food or kitchenware. I move into the bedroom Nora and her mom shared. The bed is gone, but there are clothes and shoes and personal belongings scattered around, mostly her mom's shit.

What the hell happened?

The dude taps me on the shoulder, and I nearly jump out of my skin. "Hey, we need to move." The guy is already walking down the narrow hall for the door.

When I step outside, he's waiting for me with his hand out. "Light." I reach inside the bag, pull out one of the glow sticks, and hand it to him. He cracks the middle, tossing it onto the porch, and then pulls his rifle up, striding forward. "Keep up."

I clutch onto the back of his vest, swallowing another wave of bile, desperately trying to keep in step with him.

CHAPTER TWELVE

5:08 P.M.

NORA

My eyes are glued to the door that leads up to the garage. My heart is pounding so loud I can barely hear anything else. My ears strain, trying to catch every sound, just in case it comes back. The way it ripped through the garage makes me wonder what it was searching for. Was it hunting us on our way here, or could it hear me making a video by the door?

Either way, heebie-jeebies.

"Nora!" I rush toward Mr. Gibson's weak voice.

The second I see him, I know he's worse. He's pale and slick with sweat, as if he's been on a bender. *Like Mom,* and why I thought he only needed a quick nap after all the booze he drank. But now, there's pain across his face, deep in every line and wrinkle. Something is seriously wrong with him. I really hope this isn't some new strain of COVID in the middle of all this crap.

"You aren't looking too good."

"I don't feel too good." His voice is low, different. It's

all wrong. It doesn't even seem like him. "Check my wound, will ya?"

"Sure." I carefully step closer to the bed and lift the damp sheet aside. Dark red blood, nearly black, is soaking through the dressing. I peel back the bandage, and a wave of dread courses through me. His wound is bigger and swollen, with some kind of gray pus oozing out the center of it. My gut tightens.

Is this what's making him sick?

Oh, my goodness, if it is, I don't know how to fix it. I'm no friggin' doctor.

"What is it? What's wrong?" His voice trembles.

"I don't know."

"Get the medical book." He coughs so deep, it sounds painful.

"Okay. I'll be right back." I swing myself around the doorframe, heading into the kitchen. Stopping by the table, I squat, dragging the medical tub back out. I pry off the lid, digging through the supplies.

Mr. Gibson coughs, and this time, it sounds like he's choking. "Mr. Gibson?"

Nothing. Even his choking has stopped.

"You okay in there?" I lean to my right, looking over my shoulder. He's in the hallway, clutching the wall for support.

"You shouldn't be up." I grab the medical book and push to my feet. As I walk back to him, I notice his lips are dark blue, almost black. "Let me help you back to bed."

He eyes the hatch. "I need to go. Miranda's calling for me."

My heart stops at my mom's name. *Is his fever so high he doesn't know what's going on?* A soreness pulls in my throat as I lift his arm, propping it over my shoulders. His skin is cold and clammy. I thought he had a fever.

Or is this how a fever gets when it's super high? I really wish I knew more about this stuff.

"I know. Me too, and we can go when you are better." I wrap my arm around his back, and his hands and legs shake as he tries to steady himself and walk with me.

After I help him back into bed, I flip through the medical book. I don't even know what I'm looking for. Even if I did, I don't think I could concentrate on it. His wound is really bad, and that fever, if that's what it is, I've never seen anything like it before. Not that I've seen a lot of wounds or sick people. Heck, if not for these strange monsters, all this wouldn't bother me, but now, I'm not so sure that's what it is.

Is it normal for blood to turn black like that?

Maybe that's what I should be looking for. Maybe that's why his skin is cold and feverish. I lean against the wall, flipping through the pages.

"Nora, something is wrong." I flick my eyes up, and his eyes are glazed over, darting back and forth. He pats at his chest. "I can hear your . . . " He coughs, and black spittle splatters onto his face.

I step forward, plucking a tissue out of the box on the bedside table. Before I can clean his face, he grabs my wrist, mumbling something so low I can hardly make it out.

Disbelief forces my gaze onto the wall across from me. At all the weapons arranged in their rightful places. Rifles, pistols, and even a few different sizes of machetes. I look back at Mr. Gibson. "Are you asking for a gun?"

He shakes his head, mumbling again. This time, I lean

close to his mouth. He breathes hot and wet into my ear, "Run."

I instantly straighten as fear grips me. Mr. Gibson must be really sick or hurt for him to ask me to leave without him for help.

"Let me get you some water and another blanket first." I hurry back into the kitchen and drop the book onto the counter. I pull down a plastic cup from the cabinet with worry thick in my throat. Tears pool under my eyes as I hold the cup under the faucet.

Who am I supposed to go get? The world is in chaos.

I glance up. *Is there anyone still alive?*

Mr. Gibson lets out another rattling cough.

"I'm hurrying." I focus back on the water streaming out. It looks dirty. There's a brown tint to it. *Eww.* I dump it out and refill the cup as a high-pitched shriek slices through the air.

I turn the faucet off, and the cup shakes violently. *Did one of those things get in here?*

I slowly turn around. Water sloshes over the rim of the cup.

Mr. Gibson is crouched, his back curled forward with his arms between his legs, holding himself up. He sniffs the air like one of those monsters, and his eyes are no longer hazel, but black with dark veins bulging beneath them. He opens his mouth wide and terrifying, like he's yawning awake, and black saliva drips off his teeth.

What the frig? How did he turn into one of them?

My heart hammers. Sweat coats every inch of my body as I glance at the surgical instruments we used earlier. I don't want to hurt Mr. Gibson unless I have to.

Maybe I can outrun him.

I force a hard swallow. My eyes dart from the exit to him, hunched in the hallway.

There's no way I'll make it. If he leaps, he'll have me before I can reach it. I start to move toward the table, and his black eyes focus on me. I stop at once.

He turns his head, sniffing the air again. Very quietly, I inch closer to the table. He shrills again with his attention focused on the exit. He heads toward it, awkwardly, as if he's just learned how to walk again. He grabs at the door-knob, trying to open it, but it won't budge. Then, his fist bangs against the door. With another screech, he begins clawing and hitting at it.

I lower the cup to the floor. He knew where the exit was. Could it be he's still in there? I reach over, wrapping my fingers around the scissors. The tip grazes the surface of the table. My heart jumps.

Mr. Gibson stops messing with the door. His gaze focuses on me.

I straighten my arms, holding the instrument out in front of me, as he hobbles toward me. "Mr. Gibson, stop. Please," I demand, and to my surprise, he does.

He stops near the sofa and angles his head, left and then right, like a dog trying to figure out what that sound was. And hope swells in my throat. Maybe there really is a small part of him in there. Or at least some kind of connec-tion for him to pause like this.

After what he said about taking care of me, I can't lose him now. I'm so tired of being alone, scared, and unwanted.

Snot runs down my nose as tears fall. This isn't fair. Not when I'm so close to having what most kids have. A family. I don't even need the love or support that comes with one. Just someone . . . there.

I'll even take whatever version of him this is.

With hope driving me forward, I know what I must do. I need to lock him up. I sidestep, ever so slowly, and he sniffs the air, as if my scent is hooked into his nose, guiding him in my direction. I stop and shuffle left. So does he.

He can't see me, but he can definitely smell and hear me. And with him knowing I'm in this direction, there's no way I can maneuver around him. I won't be able to lure him back into his room. He has me completely blocked in.

I glance over my shoulder for something bigger than these tiny scissors. The medical book on the counter catches my eye. Perhaps I can trick him. If I can launch the book across the room, maybe he'll chase after the noise, then I can get him into his room. I tiptoe backward, reaching for the book. When I turn around, I inhale a ragged breath. That simple, faint hum of air passing through my lips has him producing a shrill so loud, my ears throb.

I lift my hands to cup my ears and accidentally nick my chin with the instrument, and he goes into a frenzy. He barrels forward, wild, animal-like, sneezing and shrilling with each leap more violent than the next.

Oh, crap! He's fast.

I round the kitchen table, turn, and then lift the table up and over. He screeches to a halt, slamming into it. While he desperately tries to find his footing, I race around him and the table. Once in the hall, I force a glance over my shoulder, and a primal, gut-wrenching scream rips out of me.

He's coming right for me.

Fear drives me straight into his room. I turn, slamming the door onto his hands, but it doesn't faze him. He grips the edge, holding it open a crack.

"Please stop." I sob.

He pushes harder against the door, and it opens a smidge wider.

"Please, Mr. Gibson. Stop." I grip the scissors tighter. "I don't want to hurt you." My footing slides, and without thinking, I stab through the crack, over and over.

Finally, he shrieks, loosening his grip, and I'm able to fully close the door.

With shaky, sweaty hands and quick, hard pants, I manage to lock it. I lean against the door, completely alone and terrified, not knowing what my next move should be.

My body jerks forward at the force of his next attack. I glare at the weapons hanging on the wall. I know what I should do, I just don't want to do it. Mr. Gibson was all I had left besides Amy, and I don't even know if she's alive.

He shrieks again, banging and ramming against the door. It's only a matter of time before he breaks it down.

I lower my chin in a trembling fit.

I don't know if I have it in me to kill him.

COFFIN FALLS

FALLS

TRAPPED IN
FOREVER NIGHT

BOOK 2 OUT NOW!

THANK YOU!

Thank you for reading *Coffin Falls: The Day The Dome Fell*. If you enjoyed the book, I would love if you could leave a review on Amazon or Goodreads.

AMAZON

GOODREADS

ABOUT THE AUTHOR

Trena Cannon is a young adult dystopian/apocalyptic author. When not writing or spending time with her family, she can be found reading or in front of the Xbox gaming. Trena enjoys coffee, dark humor, and a good prank.

ALSO BY
TRENA CANNON

Standalone

The Edge of Hope

Coffin Falls Series

Book 1: The Day The Dome Fell

Book 2: Trapped In Forever Night

Book 3: *Coming Summer 2026*

Book 4: *Coming Fall 2026*